WHISPERS OF ADDINGTON MANOR

WHISPERS OF ADDINGTON MANOR

M. E. Hansen

Published by K&M Publishing

First published in 2021

ISBN 978-1-956167-00-9 Paperback
ISBN 978-1-956167-01-6 Ebook
ISBN 978-1-956167-02-3 EPUB

Printed in the United States of America

AUTHOR'S NOTE
This novel is a work of fiction and contains the following: moderate supernatural violence, mild gore, mild sensuality, and drinking.

Names, characters, places, and incidents are either the product of the author's imagination or are used fictitiously, and any resemblance to actual persons, living or dead, events, or locales is entirely coincidental.

I dedicate this book to my wonderful husband,
thanks for joining me on this lovely adventure
—M. E. Hansen

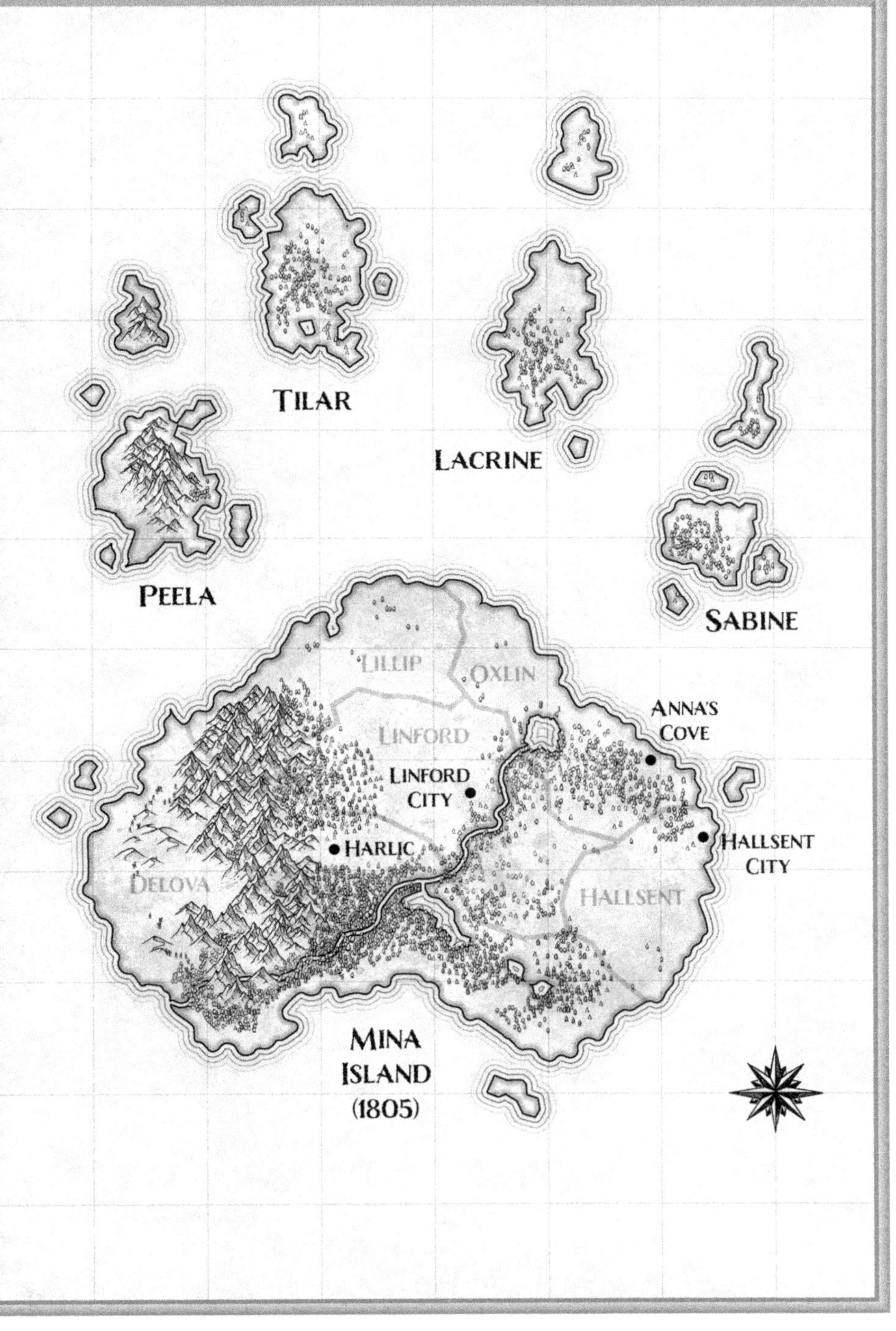

TILAR
LACRINE
PEELA
SABINE
LILLIP
OXLIN
ANNA'S COVE
LINFORD
LINFORD CITY
HARLIC
HALLSENT CITY
DELOVA
HALLSENT
MINA ISLAND
(1805)

CHAPTER 1

This is all Harold's fault.

He convinces me to set aside my fears of failure and embrace my ambitious courage to proclaim my sincere intentions to marry Miss Selene Addington. Had I ignored him, I would be home right now basking in the sunshine and reading a good book. Instead, I stand at the border where the quaint township of Anna's Cove ends and Addington Manor begins, knowing I might as well be standing upon the edge of a cliff. After a late night of drinking at Harold's family cottage, my loose lips confessed my intentions and love for Selene. This was no shock to Harold. He'd noticed a gradual lift in my mood over the past nine months and suspected a woman was to blame. He took to encouraging me to pursue my feelings, ignoring the fact that I am an accounting apprentice beneath her father, Arthur Addington.

"Here we are. Go and seize your future," my only confidant, Harold Taylor, expresses with excitement.

The unshaven brunet with dark eyes and fair skin towers over me, like most men, and places a heavy hand upon my shoulder. We stare in silence at Addington Manor as the snort of carriage horses echoes not far from us.

I run my hands through my fiery red hair and rest them at the nape of my neck. "I shouldn't be here. Master Addington specifically said—"

"Forget what he said," Harold chides. "Here before you is an opportunity to go to him, not as an apprentice, but as a man."

Harold's definition of a man differs greatly from mine, but I step away from him and lean closer to the black iron gate. Bitter excitement fills me as I contemplate what I would say to Mr. Addington. My heart races like a wild thoroughbred. I'm well acquainted with anxiety, ever since I awoke hungover in Harold's drawing room. I want to turn away and go home, but I can't allow another moment to pass by with my love for Selene going unspoken.

Harold's right. I must speak with Mr. Arthur Addington at once, for if I don't, I fear some other suitor will whisk her away.

I'm surprised it hasn't already been done.

Oh, Selene Addington. If there were a more vibrant color in the world it would bear her name. No beautiful landscape can compare to the beauty of her face. No form of entertainment could match the sharpness of her wit and the charm of her spirit. Selene fills a room with warmth by simply walking into it. Not even the grandest of starry nights mesmerize me as much as she.

It was but only two weeks ago we shared our first kiss. It was in the rose garden, beside the water fountain. She discussed her dislike about the social expectation a woman must undergo when she comes of age for marriage. By social standards, Selene would be considered a bit past her time for marriage, she being twenty-two years of age.

I, being twenty-four, never took much thought to marrying since no opportunities came to me. Growing up destitute on the streets of Linford, one didn't have much time for romance. But sitting there, the sound of bubbling water filling the air, mixing with the melodic sound of her voice, I knew I was ready to share whatever time the Blessed Creator would allow. I recall leaning in and catching her attention. She grew silent but smiled. I anticipated her stopping me, questioning my sudden change, but instead, she leaned forward, the scent of her perfume encompassing us as we shared a tender kiss.

Over the last four months, Selene and I took long walks, our conversations filled with banter of society and other secrets we dared not speak aloud. I've been an open book with her. I've shared parts of my life I wouldn't feel comfortable expressing to others. She often keeps our conversations within the boundaries of certain topics—the weather or the social mistreatment of servants and women. But occasionally she expresses her dreams of someday presenting her portraits in a Linford Gallery.

She always asks about Linford. It's the largest city on Mina Island in the providence which shares the same name. Compared to Anna's Cove with its lazy, rolling hills, quiet poppy fields, and endless meadows of sheep, Linford is busy, industrial, and always progressing. I don't miss it one bit. Though I never intended to end up in the small township of Anna's Cove, I hope never to leave unless Selene's by my side.

"It's not every day a man's affections are returned with as much passion. You cannot allow this opportunity to pass you by," Harold says, urging me to open the gate.

I agree. According to Harold, love is always the reason for everything. I think he's hiding a deeper pain. Ever since Selene's eldest sister, Elara, rejected his proposal for courtship, Harold has either drunk away his sorrows or over-entertained the notion he's all right.

He continues, "Devin, what better time to let her father know your sincerest feelings and work out a proposal of courtship, or even better, engagement? You've carried on your secret affair far too long. It's time to make it official."

I wince at the thought of Mr. Addington disapproving of my intended proposal and choosing to terminate my apprenticeship on the spot. He's a fine accountant and tends to several of the neighbor's finances, helping them save on their expenses, make wiser investments, and assure their children's allowances aren't going to waste. Over the past six months I've learned so much. Mr. Addington has expressed how impressed he is with my skills and even trusted me to tend the books of a few local clients. Though, I still have three more years before I may officially take on my own clients, I think I have a good grasp on how to manage one's wealth.

I do find it interesting how a man of his wealth and status decided on a vocation in the first place. I respect his wishes to expand beyond the social standards upheld by residents of Anna's Cove. If a man doesn't inherit his wealth through marriage or attain it by means of family profit, he is considered odd and should be spoken to with caution.

The people in Anna's Cove share the ideals of the gentry and frown upon a working man who labors for his wages. Mr. Addington doesn't agree with the thought. He claims somebody generations ago had to labor in order to accrue their family's current wealth and status. Much wealth was brought by the first settlers through mining and building, logging, and farming.

Countryside folk were always strange to me. There's too much time wasted in this quaint little township tucked away by sparse glades, and the beautiful eastern shoreline of Mina Island.

Too many frivolous conversations and speculations give life to the elderly women and bachelorettes.

In Linford one doesn't have the luxury of sitting and commenting on the weather. While the wealthy enjoy the entertainment, fine dining, and countless art galleries, everyone else is keeping the city alive. There is always work to be done.

Clenching my hands into fists, I turn and face the manor once more.

"This isn't the best time. Mr. Addington has much on his mind. I shall discuss this matter next week."

I start walking away, but Harold stops me. "You are not passing up this chance. I know how you are. You talk yourself out of accomplishing your greatness without taking a chance. You must do this. You and Selene are a perfect match. You make each other happy. I notice these things and I know love when I see it."

He turns me around, practically pushing me against the iron gate.

I know he's right. Harold is right about everything when it comes to love.

"What if Arthur rejects me? Or worse?" I ask, fiddling with the hem of my best brown suit and placing my hands within my pockets. My neck aches from how tight Harold tied my cravat, and my vest is a little snug around my chest.

Staring deep into my pale blue eyes, Harold purses his lips. "Last night you were embroiled with a fire unlike any other. Nothing could get in your way. It was you who went off on how much you wished to make Selene your wife."

I agree, but I was also quite drunk, and my ambitions were untamed. "Yes, yes, go on."

"Revive the ambitious courage. Approach Arthur, speak your intentions, and eliminate any reason for displeasure. He will not reject you. The man is as soft as a feather-filled pillow and I believe you can use this to your advantage."

I sigh. My hands are still hidden in my pockets. I don't want to risk losing this great opportunity for a decent vocation, but I can't go any longer feeling the way I do about Selene.

"But Mr. Addington said—"

"Enough. You can do this. I cannot allow my dearest friend to live in the shadow of what might have been when he has the opportunity staring him in the face."

Both of us look toward Addington Manor.

Upon first glance it's no different than any other immaculate estate in town. With dark red brick walls and black shingled roofs, the two-story house centers a well-kept yard surrounded by a stone wall. My favorite features are the many gargoyles resting at the corners of the manor, each shaped like a malformed wolf. The windowsills are also carved with wolf heads growling at one another, and above the main doors is a black iron wolf bust, its jaws gaping open in a snarl.

Toward the end of the estate, past the wide open fields of grass, is a large patch of forest claimed to have been grown by the Addington family over the past two centuries. Every spring a few more trees are planted in honor of their ancestors. But nature has also increased the reach of the woods.

I sigh, my stomach grumbling as if filled with thousands of restless butterflies. "I blame you for any mistreatment I receive because of your encouragement," I say, stepping closer to the man.

He rests a tender hand upon his heart. "Should this moment of bravery cost you your future, I will take complete blame. I'll even replace any lost wages and speak with Mr. Addington personally."

As the heir to a family winery on the mainland, of course Harold can say such things. He's living on Mina Island because his old, dying Aunt Lydia needed an extra hand around the house. I suppose it was boredom which inspired him to befriend me. He's been keeping me entertained by his wild views of society as we enjoyed each other's company. He often raves how different things are on the mainland. He finds everything about Mina Island odd, the various climates and terrains, the subtle shifts of culture from one township to another, and the shape of the island, itself. Yes, the shape of the island leaves him shaking his head each time he looks at a map. It reminds him a large, dog's paw, Mina Island being the fleshy palm, bordered by four other rocky island inhabited by nomads and convicts.

Though I've never ventured beyond the familiar townships of Linford and Anna's Cove, I'm left curious by what lies beyond this island. I suppose for now, some mysteries will remain as such.

I stare once again at the manor looming in the distance, mocking me with its majestic appearance in the morning sunlight. Keeping my hands hidden in my pockets, I clasp a few dried flower petals and think of my mother, may the Creator keep her. I should think she would have disapproved of Harold's foolish encouragement, but on the other hand, she would've also sided with him in finally expressing my intentions for Selene.

"All right. I suppose it's better to do this sober," I say, finally reaching for the gate and pulling it open.

Harold laughs. "That's the spirit. Go on."

He distances himself, a wide smile still plastered upon his face. "Now I expect you to come straight to my family cottage with the good news of your arrangement. I'll ready the wine for a celebration."

"But the time can't be later than eight in the morning," I say, wanting to make note of his issue with alcohol.

"Ah, but it's never too early to give praise to a newly engaged friend."

He motions for me to carry on, and I step further onto the drive. Making sure I'll continue my walk, he pushes the gate shut, wraps his arms around the seam, and clasps his elbows together.

"This is all your fault," I say, straightening my jacket.

"And when you are happily married, I expect you to thank me for this blessed moment."

Sighing, I turn from my friend and stroll along the freshly trimmed drive. My imagination runs wild, and I stare at the large pond in front of the manor to steady my nerves. A few servants skim the water with nets. Four fountains spring alive, adding to the fantastical view of the estate. Large oak trees line the drive, providing shade from the rising sun. The birds are already awake, singing their welcome songs and taking flight among the treetops. I say good morning to the servants, each smiling in return.

Though I'm not considered a servant, according to Mr. Addington, I am a man of lesser station. I arrived in Anna's Cove nine months ago, shortly after my mother's passing, with a decent amount of money in my pocket but nothing more to my name than a history of poverty and woe. I took on odd jobs, residing in a room above the local pub, using my money to pay for rent and to purchase some nice suits. I remained there for a few months, until one day I was approached by a tall man dressed in a fine suit and top hat.

It was Mr. Arthur Addington, the wealthiest man in Anna's Cove.

"I'm in need of an apprentice in the vocation of accounting," he said, his voice deep but kind. "The opportunity will last a few years, assuming you'll be dedicated with your studies."

The complexion of his skin reminded me of the golden sheen of beer when the sun hits a glass just right. He smelled like a pub but was as sober as a priest on All Saint's Day.

"I know how to read and count, but I don't know much about money and tending to it," I replied.

Arthur smiled, his dark eyes reflecting the sun's light. "The fact you understand what accounting entails is good enough for me."

I wasn't sure why he selected me. Perhaps it was because I wasn't local and tainted by the ideals of Anna Cove's society. Maybe he took pity on my impoverished state. Regardless, my mother always expressed how one should never turn down an opportunity of great wealth and status.

And before the week was done, I moved from the dingy room above the pub into the old miller's cottage Mr. Addington had purchased months earlier. These past six months have been delightful, not only enriching my life in the knowledge of numbers and wealth, but also in love. I can only hope to appeal to Arthur's generous heart when it comes to the topic of his daughter.

"Good morning to you, Mr. Foster," one of the servants calls from the yard. He waves from his grass cutter.

"Same to you Brandon," I say, calming my trembling voice.

I continue down the drive, kicking up dust. My heart races

with each step closer to the manor.

Four more servants are tending to the ferns in front of the manor, one scrubbing the stone vases the foliage grows from. Everything must be perfect for the engagement celebration tonight. Arthur's youngest son, Marcus, was recently engaged to Miss Diane Kendall. The manor has been bustling all week in preparation for the event tonight.

I pause, turning toward the pond and taking a deep breath. If I gain Arthur's approval, it would only be a matter of time before I am engaged to Selene. I'm certain she loves me. Every secret kiss, invigorating conversation, and moment spent together shows me I am not a fool.

I must remain confident. Despite perhaps losing every opportunity of progress, the next worst thing Arthur could do is simply reject the idea and tell me to go home.

With another sigh I continue, trusting Harold's confidence in me as I near the front door.

CHAPTER 2

I rap my knuckles against the dark oak door, hoping it's loud enough. I stand awkwardly waiting, my palms growing sweaty. The soft sound of music attempts its escape through a nearby window. I don't think I was heard. I decide to use the heavy knocker for a more robust knock. Grasping the black ring within a wolf's mouth, I tap three times and wait.

"Mr. Foster, why don't you enter as usual?" one of the gardening servants asks. She fans herself with her wide brim hat and sits near a bowl of blue zinnias. "Mr. Brent and the footmen are probably too busy tending to all the preparations for tonight."

"I believe you're right, Ms. Henders. But I'm willing to wait today," I say, squinting from the morning sun.

Since becoming Mr. Addington's apprentice, I've been given permission to come and go as I please, as long as I arrive and leave during my expected times and enter only Mr. Addington's study, the library, and the waiting room.

I stand a little longer at the door before knocking once

again. This time, Mr. Jamison Brent, the butler, pulls open the door, raises his eyebrows, and parts his lips.

"Mr. Foster, you're not expected at the manor. Is there something I can do for you?"

I choke on my words, unsure what to say. "I—I'm here . . . to speak with Mr. Addington."

The old man steps outside, closes the door behind him, and stares me down with his pale gray eyes. His face is long and thin, like the rest of his body, and lined with spindly wrinkles. His bald head reflects the sun's rays as he folds his arms across his chest, wrinkling his black, pressed suit.

"Why have you arrived unannounced? Mr. Addington specifically told you to not return until next week."

My heart races. "I—I know, but—"

We stand in silence. I peer over the well-manicured grounds, debating if I should share my intentions with Mr. Brent. I trust he can keep a secret. Often, I've noticed his stern scowl whenever Selene and I read in the library unchaperoned. I'm sure he's had his moments of wanting to report to Mr. Addington of my conduct with Selene but chose not to. He's a good man, always showing the utmost respect to everyone he serves, especially me. I've grown accustomed to Mr. Brent's gruff looks; I don't think the man knows how to express any other emotion besides disappointment and surprise. He's always guarded and concerned for the well-being of the family, and I respect him for it.

I gather my wits once again and lean closer to conceal my important secret.

"My reasoning to come concerns Miss Selene, but I wish to make such information known to Mr. Addington personally. I only request a moment of his time, fearing the outcome, due to the nature of my intended conversation."

The old man doesn't flinch. His eyes study me, his lips pursing to a thin frown.

"Mr. Addington is speaking with his brother, Alfred, at the moment. I will allow you inside, but you must wait until I know for certain Mr. Addington is available."

A wave of relief overcomes me, and I follow him inside. "Thank you, Mr. Brent."

He escorts me around several servants dusting the decorative fixtures or scrubbing the white tiled floor.

Following at a respectable distance, I stop abruptly when Mr. Brent is interrupted by an inquisitive servant. I care little of their conversation and am overwhelmed by the grandeur of the open lobby. I'm always amazed at the sight of the two grand staircases mirroring one another as they ascend to the next floor. The towering walls are decorated with gold framed portraits. White marble statues of thin animals fill every corner.

The smell of freshly baked sweet cakes fills the air as the clang of pots and pans and servants' shouts echo from the kitchen down the grand hallway. Oh, how I love the taste of sweet cakes.

Today, a large table is placed dead center of the open space and topped with an enormous porcelain vase. I assume it will be filled with beautiful foliage and flowers before the guests arrive tonight. At either side of the table are servants standing upon ladders, dusting the lowered grand chandelier and carefully replacing the four hundred candles within their metal cups. It would be a shame if drops of hot wax were to fall upon Mrs. Addington's arriving guests, so each are precise in balancing the white candles with care.

Unknowingly, I tap my hand against my side, paying little attention to Mr. Brent speaking with the servant. To my left are a few servants dusting several shelves in the waiting room. It's a cozy place with two sofas and a few chairs surrounding a quaint fireplace. Just about every room has a fireplace. I suspect Mr. Brent will escort me there to wait as he speaks with Mr. Addington, but to my surprise he ushers me into the parlor instead.

"I will return as soon as possible," he says, his cheeks now a little flushed from the conversation. I hope everything's all right.

I stand in the parlor, holding my hands behind my back.

Two servants are busy dusting the many wooden chairs and fluffing sofa pillows. They mind their business as a sullen tune plays from the piano pressed against the far wall.

Elara Addington's delicate fingers move along the keys gracefully, expressing a tune of passion gone wrong. Her long blonde hair is pulled into a low ponytail and braided with black and green ribbons. She pays little attention to the servants and makes the music swell with an intense crescendo. I'd be a fool to not be moved by the sad song, but I'm also not surprised to hear such an etude brought to life by Elara's hands.

"There we have it," an old servant says, clapping his hands free of excess soot as he admires the fresh logs he's fashioned into a small square in the fireplace. He lifts a metal basket with old, ashen wood, trying not to spill its filthy contents.

One of the dusting servants glances at the display and smiles her approval before carrying on to the various bookshelves built into the wall.

"That will be all, Mr. Andrews," Elara says without missing a note. "Please be sure to sweep the soot before you leave and don't forget the floor cloth."

"Yes, Miss Elara. My apologies." Embarrassed, the servant bows and returns to his duties in silence.

I silently stare at Miss Addington and listen to her play the sad melody. She's Selene's eldest sister and, unlike most of the Addingtons children, Elara looks exactly like her mother, a woman of fair complexion, golden blonde hair, and is so thin I sometimes question whether she eats enough food. Elara is mostly silent, but when she speaks her tone is not the least bit pleasant. I'm sure her voice is beautiful, if only she lightened it up a bit when speaking to others.

"And what brings you here, Mr. Foster?" Elara asks, glancing over her shoulder and playing the final notes of her song.

I part my lips to explain, but she abruptly stands and saunters my way with a devious smirk on her face. "Does it have to do with my sister?" She lifts an eyebrow and folds her arms across her chest.

I'm baffled. So much so that I glance at the front door wondering if she somehow heard my whispering with Mr. Brent. It's impossible. Nothing so soft spoken could have been heard between the melodic music and excited shouts from the servants. Plus, the door was closed. Maybe a window was open, of which I'm not aware.

She stops a few feet away from me, her dark jade dress swishing with her pause. I've never seen her wear anything but dark colors. Though always elegant, the clothes she wears give the impression she's in mourning. Everyone else in the family wears lighter colors all year round. But not Elara.

"Why do you assume I'm here because of Selene?" I ask, feeling my cheeks warm.

Her smirk deepens. "You're wearing your best suit." Her dark eyes move from my head to my feet, narrowing as she looks over my shined shoes. I remain silent, not surprised by her prying eyes.

"There's no other reason for you to arrive unannounced." Her face softens. "Unless you forgot your ledger and needed to make some important note for a client, in which case you must also be on your way to some special occasion."

Again, I make no indication to prove whether she is right or wrong. I peek at the lobby, hoping Mr. Brent will return soon.

Elara continues. "Besides, I would be lying if I claimed I haven't notice you and Selene prancing about the manor these past couple weeks. Selene's face lights up whenever you arrive for work. I may remain quiet most of my days, but I am not dumb. You have an influence on my sister. It's her flaw, allowing men to manipulate her emotions and toy with her heart."

I'm elated to know I bring a sense of joy to Selene whenever I'm not around but offended by Elara assuming my intentions to be devious.

"I assure you, any interactions between Miss Selene and I

are strictly of a friendly nature. I would never bring sadness or pain to anyone in this family. It is not my intention to manipulate, nor do I believe I'm capable of such a feat."

This prompts a distrusting sneer from the woman. She steps closer, her dark brown eyes narrowing with each step. "You must understand that, whatever your intentions are with my sister, they will not come to pass. We Addingtons marry for wealth and status, not for love. Know this, my father will never approve of your courtship."

I try to humor the woman, knowing clearly what is to be expected of me should I gain Mr. Addington's blessing. He provides me a modest allowance, a third of which it I've saved, yet I won't be able to settle upon a decent arrangement. Engagements are opportunities to assure the intended woman will be well taken care of financially. Should the intended man not have the finances to provide, he's given a year to save enough money to meet the price the father's expectations. I find it ridiculous, but in the same vein, I respect such precautions. Nobody wishes to enter a marriage agreement on a shaky financial foundation.

"Marcus and Diane appear to be in love," I say, taking a step away from the thin woman.

This remark doesn't bode well with Elara, and she answers tepidly, "Because wealthy men are free to do as they please. Besides, the Kendalls have always accrued great wealth by marrying wisely. Marcus is lucky to enjoy the pleasures of both love and money."

I check the door, wishing Mr. Brent would return. Elara's deep glare sends shivers into the depths of my soul.

"Speaking of engagements," I say, forcing a happy smile, "I don't believe I've officially congratulated you on your engagement to Mr. Bottrell. Harold, on the other hand, offers his condolences upon the death of a happy union. He wasn't specific on which union." I pause to stop my rambling. For a moment, Elara's demeanor lightens with the mention of Harold, but only for a mere moment.

She balls her hands into fists. Her whole body tenses. With a forced smile, she turns her attention to the window. "Yes, thank you. If everything goes well with Mr. Bottrell, we'll be married come this autumn. There are a few arrangements left to be settled, namely where we will live."

"I hear he has a few cottages on the mainland. Mr. Bottrell truly is a man with much means. Wonderful conversationalist."

Talking about Mr. Bottrell makes her uncomfortable. I won't lie. Part of me is satisfied with matching her stinging remarks, but deep down, I pity her. Quiet, conservative, Elara Addington would be considered a woman of tradition—dull, tedious tradition.

Harold tried to court her, but she rejected his advances without explanation. He says she was a bore, never once indulging in social drinking or dancing, and keeping mostly to her piano and violin. He often speaks ill of those who frown upon his wild living, but with Elara, he never speaks harsher words than that. In fact, whenever Harold reflects over his time spent chasing after her, his eyes gaze off into the distance as if searching for a happiness he could have had by her side.

I blame Elara for Harold's increasingly terrible habits, especially his drinking. He rarely entered the pub when I worked there, but shortly after his rejection, he and I frequented the establishment at least two or three times a week. His aunt disapproves of his causal drinking at home, and he trusts I will assure his safety when traveling home late at night. The horrible effects women have upon us men.

Elara doesn't respond to my comment about Mr. Bottrell's wealth. She isn't given time because Mr. Brent enters the parlor, his forehead a little moist, perhaps from all the scurrying he's been doing all morning.

"Mr. Addington will see you now."

CHAPTER 3

Mr. Brent escorts me up the grand staircase. A few servant girls holding decorative bowls and towels walk toward Selene's room, flashing friendly smiles in my direction. Hattie, Selene's personal maidservant, gives a quick nod and ushers the other servants around the corner.

Hattie was the first of many servants who spoke with me and helped with anything I needed.

I'm not one to accept service from the servants. I tend to my own needs whenever I'm working at the manor. I fetch my own drinks or plates of food, but on occasion, Mr. Addington reminds me I'm more of a guest and should allow the servants to do their jobs, respecting their dignity. Most of the servants work here to avoid the poor houses. Some were brought here at a young age, dropped off by their parents with hopes of better prospects. Some were in search of work and offered their services in exchange for a roof over their heads and any amount of wages Mr. Addington was willing to pay.

"Keep up, Mr. Foster, please. I have much to do today. I mustn't waste any more time with this spontaneous situation you've concocted in your head."

I follow quickly, keeping in step, moving farther down the hall. I pass a few potted plants, practically stepping over a servant who adds more dirt to one.

"Sorry, Mr. Foster," the young boy says.

"It's all right, Thomas, nothing to worry about. Continue on," I say, smiling.

The grand hallway is filled with light streaming into it from the adjacent rooms. Upon this level are the family and servant living quarters, the library, the recreation room, and Mr. Addington's study. And though guests are never allowed upstairs during hosted celebrations, Mrs. Addington always insists every inch of the manor be cleaned to her approval.

The energy of servants dusting, scrubbing, laughing, and talking fills me with a sense of joy. The servants at Addington Manor are happy and grateful to be working here. I hear how they speak about the family, and despite their occasional negative discussion of Mrs. Addington's views about the lower-class, they have only the best words concerning Mr. Addington. My admiration grows more and more for him, and I hope to one day be the kind of thoughtful man he is. One can tell a lot about a privileged family by how content their servants are.

We finally reach Mr. Arthur Addington's study. Its location is in a dead-end hallway with a single window accenting a grand clock pressed against a wall. I listen to the rhythmic ticking, waiting patiently to speak with Arthur. There are no vases or end tables or plants in this hallway—the way he likes it, thus no reason for servants to disrupt him and his eldest brother, Alfred.

I find the door slightly ajar and can hear Arthur conversing with Alfred. Though I've never personally met Alfred, I've been told he is quite set in his ways in defining what constitutes a proper Addington.

Selene can't stand him. She disagrees with his views toward

women. He only praises those who pander to the social ideal. And though he's never married, supposedly due to his foul temper, he always reminds Selene and Elara what he thinks makes for a proper wife.

I step closer to the door, but Mr. Brent insists I keep my distance. We wait for the opportune moment to enter, since the men are obviously in a heated conversation.

I peer through the small seam into the study, seeing Arthur leaning against his desk, staring at his brother, who stands away from my view. Besides the family library, Arthur's study is my favorite room. There's a wall filled with educational books, their spines promising knowledge of philosophy, religion, science, and, of course, accounting and mathematics. I could spend my days perusing the personal collection and still have more questions about life and whatever is beyond it. Sometimes Arthur allows me to sit in front of the fireplace and read whatever I wish. Sometimes he joins me.

I smile at the thought of us reading before a roaring fire after a few hours of balancing books for clients. But my happy thoughts are interrupted when Alfred walks toward the windows. The morning light accents his dark eyes and weathered face. He's taller than Arthur, and his voice is much deeper.

"If you lived in Hallsent, we wouldn't be having this discussion," Alfred says, his tone harsh and sharp.

"Brother, I am content to remain here in Anna's Cove and within this house. Besides, there's so much growth in Oxlin Providence. A university will be built a few towns over in the coming years."

"Yes, and I suppose you'll get a real education from it," Alfred says, facing his brother.

Arthur shakes his head and runs a hand through his dark brown hair. All Addington men are tall with a tan complexion, accentuating their dark brown eyes. And though Arthur's height and broad stature can appear intimidating, he has the gentlest appearance to him, no matter his emotional state. Even now, in his frustration with Alfred, the man looks as though he'd cry instead of yell with rage.

"I don't understand why you care so much about what I do with my life and my family," Arthur says, still leaning against his desk.

Alfred grips the bridge of his nose before raising his hands in the air along with his voice. "Because I am an Addington, and that actually means something to me. Ever since Father died, you've changed. You were once so thoughtful of keeping our name sacred, but now, you don't seem to care what people think, and I'm unsettled by it. Our father expected more from you. If he were alive—"

"He's not alive, and I am a better man for it. I grew weary from the weight of expectations he placed upon me—upon us— and now I have the freedom to do what I wish. I've pursued my dreams without the scornful looks and spiteful comments. I don't need them from you."

Alfred takes in a deep breath. "You are not worthy of the Addington name. You put to shame centuries of men who did what was necessary to maintain our wealth and status."

"I uphold such things with respect. It is not a disgrace to want to earn my own wages."

"It is a disgrace and should be done away with immediately!"

Alfred's voice fills every corner of the room, causing a passing servant to stop and stare. Mr. Brent ushers her along and rolls his eyes.

I don't agree with Alfred's opinion of Arthur's choices. I've always thought Arthur showed the utmost respect to his family name by how he conducts himself in public and never speaks ill of his father. I've been told the man was heartless and most demanding of his children.

"Perhaps this isn't a good time after all," Mr. Brent says stepping away, but I stop him, wanting to hear more of the conversation.

Alfred continues to speak. "Do you honestly think taking on

an apprentice will bring some justification of your actions? Do you believe you're doing this poor Mr. Foster a great service? People aren't going to trust him to watch over their assets and investments just because you say he's an honorable man. Nobody will hire him. I'm surprised Eliza approves of this."

The mention of Mrs. Addington makes my guts grumble. The woman is kind to only those she deems worthy of her presence. She's never approved of Arthur's actions, but in accordance with the expectations of high-society women, she supports her husband with little contention.

"I don't need Eliza's approval. I am the man of the house," Arthur says, his brow furrowed.

"Yes, but she faces the social repercussions of your actions. She shared with me how difficult it is to keep up appearances of social prowess when you took a stranger off the streets, gave him money and shelter, and allow him to come and go each day as he pleases. Mr. Foster could be a charlatan weaseling his way into the family. I've been told he takes long walks with Selene throughout the estate. It's improper for a man of his status to be doing such a thing."

Arthur tries to speak up, but Alfred continues. "Selene's fraternizing with a strange outsider diminishes her prospect immensely. Eliza tells me she hasn't had a suitor in months, nor been invited to any social gatherings. It is the way of society. How will she find a good matching? Her time is already running short."

I never thought I could be to blame for Selene's lack of social exposure. She and I are never seen outside the boundaries of Addington Manor, so more eligible suitors should not be dissuaded.

I wonder if Selene has been rejecting any possible suitors since my arrival. Has she had an eye for me all this time?

I can't help but smile and can hardly contain my thoughts. I step a little closer, leaning in as Alfred continues his rant.

"What do you even know about Mr. Foster? What makes

you feel sympathetic toward him? Clearly, he's manipulated your senses for you give him such a generous allowance along with shelter in the family cottage."

"It's the old miller's cottage—"

"Yes, a property which should be intended for Marcus and his bride."

"He's already settled with a few servants in a small chateau on the outskirts of Anna's Cove," Arthur says. "Diane has agreed to reside there after the wedding."

Alfred's tone rises, his disapproval growing louder and louder. "I don't like it, Arthur! I don't like it one bit, and I demand you put an end to all of this."

Arthur springs from his desk. He stands close to his brother, their eyes meeting with accompanying scowls and tensed jaws.

"I did not invite you into my home to lecture me on the choices I am making," Arthur says. "I will not allow this conversation to continue. I'm not worried about Mr. Foster. He's been an exemplary young man and will be prepared, as I have been, in his pursuit of a greater future. I will continue to instruct him for a few more years before he is able to take on his own business. He's a fast learner, and these past six months have proven his abilities to be good."

Never in my life has anyone spoken so boldly on my behalf.

Alfred steps out of my view. "You have no need to be an accountant; you have your wealth and status as a gentleman," he says.

I hold my breath, anticipating Arthur's response. The kind man's shoulders slump a little and he sighs. "I'm doing what I want. I have many clients who entrust me with overseeing their investments, and I have proven myself profitable. The men in this town don't frown upon my decisions. If anything, it's the women who chitter like chickens out for their morning feed."

Alfred chuckles. "The men are only being kind. I'm sure they speak ill of you behind your back."

"Then let them speak," Arthur shouts. "It doesn't matter.

Everyone residing in this wretched town cares only about wealthy associations and the status of their neighbor. I find such a belief repulsive and unnecessary. Whispers, they call them. Silent scandals nobody wishes to openly address, and yet they still maintain a social rapport despite what they really think."

I finally release my breath in a long loud exhale, catching Arthur's attention.

Panicking, I motion for Mr. Brent to enter as Arthur proceeds toward the door.

Mr. Brent complies, stepping inside and bowing. "Mr. Addington, Mr. Foster is here to speak with you."

Arthur motions me into the room. Respectfully, I enter, bow to both men, and stand, locking my knees and hiding my hands behind my back.

"Mr. Foster, I'm surprised you're here," Arthur says, forcing a pleasant smile. "May I ask why you've arrived when I gave you the day off?"

I nod, still trying not to stare at Alfred, who now sits in one of the armchairs beside the fireplace. Behind him is my working desk, untouched and well organized, as I left it yesterday. Alfred stares at me with a deep frown and eyebrows as straight as a shelf. He leans closer to me as if anticipating I will say something incredibly important. I'm sure he objects to my presence but cannot voice it due to Arthur inviting me into his office.

I clear my throat, feeling quite hot at the moment. "Yes, Mr. Addington, I have . . . come to speak with you about . . . a personal matter." Again I glance at Alfred, addressing him directly. "With all due respect, Mr. Addington, I hoped I could speak with your brother privately."

My words must spark some interest for both men exchange surprised glances.

Alfred sits up in the chair, placing his meaty hands on his knees. "Whatever business you have to speak of can be addressed before me as well. There is nothing too private I wouldn't hear about eventually."

My heart begins to pound against my ribs. This isn't what I planned. Of course, I didn't plan anything. This is all Harold's idea. I'm foolish to believe any of his ideas would work. Why did I allow him to talk me into this?

Turning to Arthur, I hope he will say something to quiet my growing nerves, but instead he asks, "Mr. Foster, why have you come?"

At this moment, so many thoughts race through my head. So many questions. So many scenarios and possibilities. So many ways this moment can go terribly wrong.

I swallow hard and take a deep breath. Why is it difficult to breathe?

I must calm down.

"Devin," Arthur speaks respectfully, "what is it you wish to tell me?"

CHAPTER 4

In a perfect situation, Arthur would welcome me with open arms after discussing my intentions with his daughter. He would acknowledge how long he'd been waiting for this moment and smile greatly. Even Alfred would be happy. We would talk about saving up for the wedding and the first year of marriage then Arthur would happily raise my allowance and give me the details on Selene's dowry. We would sit. We would laugh. We would go over the engagement contract and travel to the local magistrate to receive his stamp of approval.

Yes, in a perfect situation, I would officially be ready to ask Selene for her hand with the utmost support and encouragement of her father.

But my life has never been perfect. I was never given the opportunity to love who I pleased and live how I wished. In Linford my mother and I did everything we could to survive. We didn't have much to begin with, and my father's gaming addiction destroyed us. He died in a brawl over gambling when

I was sixteen years old. For years, my mother did what she could to keep us fed and sheltered, but as time passed, she grew weary and ill.

I tended to her, never once complaining about the twists and turns our lives had taken. Though within the shadows of my heart, I never forgot the death of my father and the torment it brought.

I still recall the feeling of his hot blood soaking my shirt as he lay in my arms, dying. I remember making a vow never to be like him. I promised myself I wouldn't die in the streets, unsure of where I was or who I was with. I tried to comfort the old man. He took one last look into my cold, blue eyes and brushed my cheek. He smirked. "You were never my son," he said. "Never."

Whether it was a confession, or a cruel encouragement, I didn't want to know. I never asked my mother what he could have meant.

His body grew stiff in my arms as the life left him. I sat there upon the cold stone, feeling a sense of relief and bitterness. How could he? How could he think only of himself and not about us? I'm still angered, knowing he had the chance to change his ways but refused.

"Mr. Foster, please, what is it that you need?" Arthur's voice speaks, breaking me from my thoughts.

I swallow once again and peer toward my desk. "Forgive me, yes, last night I couldn't sleep. I remembered a mistake I made with Mr. Harrow's account, and I needed to return first thing this morning to fix it. I wasn't sure if it's considered proper to speak such matters before anyone else, since you specifically expressed the confidence we place upon our clients' investments."

It is a lie. And I am a fool for speaking it.

Arthur's face softens, and he motions to my desk. "Well, dear man, I agree confidentiality is important, but I don't believe Alfred will be mentioning anything to Mr. Harrow."

This prompts the brothers to chuckle, dissipating the tense mood in the room. Arthur walks to his armchair and sits across from Alfred.

I remain standing, feeling Mr. Brent's glaring eyes burning into the back of my neck. He stands in the doorway, waiting for me. He's a busy man, and having to escort me here only to fail at my goal is probably ruining his day.

"Go right ahead and fix what you need. Mr. Brent, do wait outside. Mr. Foster shouldn't take long," Arthur says, motioning for me to move and excusing Mr. Brent at the same time. Alfred's eyes narrow at the notion.

I shuffle toward my desk, open my ledger, and flip through the pages. I'm not sure how long I should pretend to be busy. I stare at all the numbers, thousands of them.

Mr. Harrow is one of the local farmers, incompetent when it comes to large numbers. He's one of three clients Arthur is allowing me to oversee. I'm to help Mr. Harrow search for ways he can gain a profit and build a savings. The other day I spoke with the grain fetters and discovered they were charging Mr. Harrow twice as much for their labor as they would any other farmer. They blamed his lack of intelligence. Thus, I spoke with Mr. Harrow and explained what price he should be demanding, saving him an additional two hundred a month.

Alfred clears his throat and rests in the comfy chair. "I suppose we should discuss Quintin and the woman he brought with him."

I take my time turning another page. Selene never went into details about her eldest brother, only mentioning how five years ago he left without a word. There was some personal disagreement between he and Arthur that drove Quintin to leave. He arrived unannounced earlier this week with his new bride.

"Having Quintin home is delightful, and I'm excited for the newest addition to our family."

Alfred lets out a disappointed sigh. "She has no wealth or status—"

"Neither did Quintin when he first met her. I assumed he was dead up until two days ago, so please allow me to savor a decent moment of joy at his return. I think my daughter-by-law is lovely."

"Eliza isn't happy about Sophia, and I don't blame her," Alfred says. "The estranged son has arrived home after five years of absence with an impoverished new bride. But perhaps your neighbors will prefer to talk about how her skin is much darker than expected of an Addington. The old hens will be clucking for weeks."

I stand as still as possible, wondering how Arthur will react to such a comment. Most people in Anna's Cove are fair skinned and burn in the sun. Even I have moments of turning a few shades of pink and peeling for days. Sophia's exotic complexion will surely cause a stir among the socialites.

"Sophia is a good match for Quintin. She supports his carpentry while she sells vegetables and wildflowers from their garden," Arthur says in a cheerful tone.

I'm certain Arthur speaks truthfully, for being troubled by the mention of another's race is completely understandable in his society. He wouldn't lie for my benefit.

"Are you about finished, Mr. Foster?" Alfred asks, peeking over the side of the chair.

"Just about," I say, closing my ledger and replacing it inside my desk.

I face the gentlemen and respectfully nod. "Thank you for allowing me to correct my mistake."

Arthur rises and escorts me out. "It's what I admire the most about you, your keen sense of honesty. Now, do hurry away. I wouldn't want the business of this day to keep you from the lovely weather."

I step into the hallway as Arthur waves goodbye and shuts the door.

Mr. Brent's pale eyes narrow to thin slits. "And how is Mr. Harrow's account?"

I walk with the butler away from the door and into the grand hallway. "I'm truly sorry. I couldn't do it. I only have myself to blame—as well as Harold.”

“Mr. Taylor? What does he have to do with all this?”

I shake my head. “Nothing.” I want to go home now and wallow in my foolishness until my return next week for a proper day of work.

But as Mr. Brent and I enter the main hallway, we are abruptly stopped by Selene Addington.

“Selene,” I say louder than I expected, catching the attention of surrounding servants.

Her dark brown eyes stare into mine, and I’m frozen with surprise. It’s a strange reaction she induces in me, especially when she has her hair pinned up, showcasing her long neck and narrow shoulders. Small flowers are woven into a crown among her tight, chestnut curls, matching her dress. Today she wears a pastel yellow, high-waisted dress with white lace lining her seams and hems. Her tan complexion is accentuated against the light color, giving her the appearance of a sun goddess.

“Mr. Foster,” she says, her smile spreading widely across her beautiful face. “I wasn’t expecting to see you until next week.” She playfully chuckles and taps me with a book she’s holding.

My tongue is tied, and I can’t respond immediately. My voice stutters, making her laugh a little more.

“Mr. Brent,” Selene says, assertively, “I believe Ms. Whitaker needs your attention in the kitchen. One of the flues is blocked.”

Immediately the butler excuses himself.

Selene waits for him to disappear down the stairs before flashing me a devious smile.

“Do accompany me to the library,” she says, her voice soft and breathy. “I must replace this book at once.” She motions across the hallway, her curls bouncing with each movement of her head. “Unless you have something more pressing at this moment.”

There’s a certain look Selene gives me which makes my

palms sweat. The honorable man within me would choose to ignore it and insist I take my leave, but I cannot help myself. I am bewitched by the sight of her.

"I have no engagements today and will happily join you in the library," I say, steadying my trembling voice.

She leads me to the large room, giggling with delight.

When we enter the library, the smell of wood polish fills my nostrils. Morning sunlight streams from bare windows, filling each cushioned alcove with a welcoming warmth. To my left is a second level accessed by two small staircases. Shelves of educational books are there, collecting dust. To my right is an open space with plenty of armchairs and wooden seats for reading. A second doorway leads to the servant quarters and is currently shut.

Selene once explained to me that since guests aren't allowed upstairs, Mr. Addington decided to move his house servants above the ballroom. The old servant quarters are now used as cellars for food storage.

"I took the book from the balcony," Selene says, making her way to one of the narrow staircases. "Come."

Servants tend to come and go through the library, but with everyone so busy today, Selene and I are completely alone.

"I believe it belongs somewhere over here near the back," she says, hurrying toward the farthest wall. I reach the balcony and feel a tightening in the pit of my stomach.

She stops and thumbs through the various spines, humming a cheerful tune. Peeking over her shoulder, I glimpse a playful smile gracing her delicate mouth. My cheeks warm and my shoulders stiffen. A few days ago, we hid in this very spot, holding one another in a secret embrace. The excitement of sharing a forbidden kiss was almost too much for me to handle. Under different circumstances, reenacting such a moment would be tantalizing, but I fear my anxious thoughts won't allow me to savor my beloved's presence. Reluctantly, I make my way beside her and look over the books on the shelves, mostly philosophy and anatomy.

"Where exactly does your book belong?" I ask, curious about the volume she holds.

Selene stops abruptly and tosses the book on a nearby end table. In the sunlight, her eyes shimmer along with her smooth skin.

"It doesn't belong up here at all," she says.

Playfully, she pushes me against the shelves. She leans in, her voice low and quiet. "I took it from the parlor after Elara told me you'd arrived."

I see my reflection in her dark eyes and steady my racing heart. She brushes her lips against mine, puckering them into a coy smile. "Too much time has passed with you entering my thoughts." Her fingertips tug at my cravat, as she gently nibbles on my ear.

"Is that so?" I squeak, trying to maintain my composure.

She presses a gentle kiss on my cheek. "When my father explained why you weren't coming in today, I felt as though time had drawn to a complete stop. Having to wait so long to see you wrenched my heart, and I feared it would sever in two."

My dearest Selene. She has a strange way of expressing her thoughts—almost poetic.

Her fingers move along my collar, playing with the ends of my hair. They rest on my shoulders as our cheeks press against one another.

"I couldn't pass the opportunity to see you once again."

Our eyes meet and she kisses me.

If this day began on a better path, I would have happily returned my natural affections. Unfortunately, Alfred's scathing words echo in my mind. He thinks I'm a charlatan manipulating my way into the family. It's not true. I genuinely love Selene and respect Mr. Addington. I'm nothing like those who would willingly take advantage of others. If only I could prove it.

"Is something wrong?" she asks. A troubled look washes over her.

At the moment I want to confess everything to her. I want to express how I doubt my worthiness of her hand and fear her father's disapproval. But I can't. I can't do it.

"I'm sorry. There's much on my mind," I manage to say without looking at her. My body remains tense, and my heart still races.

She takes my hands, intertwining our fingers. She thinks for a moment, her eyes gazing into the ether before her smile returns. "I know what will cheer your spirits."

"I doubt it," I say. My embarrassment radiates from my hot skin.

"It will. I promise."

Leaving her book behind, she pulls me toward the nearest staircase and into the open space below.

"What do you have in mind?" I ask, not necessarily wanting to know.

We stop at the doorway, and she flashes me a mysterious expression. "An adventure, Mr. Foster." Her voice deepens. "One that will someday save your life."

CHAPTER 5

If danger lurked behind everything Selene said with a mysterious tone, my life would be in peril whenever we go for a walk. She somehow makes every venture feel like a great escape or as if I'm living a story she read in a book. Normally I eagerly indulge her, adding my own flare for the dramatic, but I'm not feeling particularly imaginative at the moment.

We enter the recreation room, and Selene requests I wait as she prepares a pleasant surprise. The room is large and filled with several sofas and armchairs. A grand fireplace gives home to the main chimney, its mantle topped with decorative vases and framed landscapes of the sea. Though used for entertainment and accommodating many guests at once, the recreation room is not especially extravagant. However, there is a particular painting hanging above the mantle, which always makes me pause and stare for a moment.

Framed in gold, the painting portrays a manlike beast standing in the full moon's light. The beast takes up most of the canvas with its broad shoulders and pointed ears. It appears to reach out, ready to snatch you up if you stand too close. The definition of the humanoid's muscles and vicious teeth are remarkable. Each brush stroke accentuates the mangled black fur covering the creature's body. The brilliance of the moon and how the light falls upon the monster fills me with a sense of awe. The unnatural red eyes captivate me. There is something intimidating about the monster's stare, as if it is stalking me, waiting for me to make a wrong move and fall victim to its powerful bite.

It's best to admire the painting from afar. It feels out of place, unnecessary among the refined décor, but I believe that's why it's here. Perhaps the intention of the painting is to grab the spectator's attention. I've heard stories of men transforming into vicious creatures within the full moon's light, but assumed such tales were metaphors for abuse or power. The creature, centered in its moonlit setting, represents a warning. Seeing the painting always makes me a little nervous from what it could represent. One should never cross an Addington.

"I'm almost ready," Selene says.

I pay little attention to her, and continue to stare at the painting, noticing the excellent craftsmanship in each stroke.

I near it, curious about the artist. In the lower right corner a familiar signature is scrawled in black ink.

"Selene, you painted this piece?" I acknowledge and point at the signature.

She finishes putting a folding table away in the far corner and joins me. "I did. Did I never mention it? It represents Henry Addington, my direct ancestor by many generations," she says. I suspect she'd be proud, but her smile is replaced with a weary frown.

Surprised by the response, I smirk. "Your great ancestor was a man beast? A monster?"

Selene doesn't look away from the unnatural creature. "Clearly my depiction is metaphorical. With his family, Henry was a kind, happy man, upholding the traditions and standards he expected his family to abide by. But as I read journals and learned more about my family's heritage, I discovered how Henry was quite monstrous to some people. He was strict and unforgiving with those who crossed him. I'm still not sure what to think about him, so I painted the vilest creature I could imagine." She pauses and chuckles. "Man beasts are quite the legend, representing a range of horrible things. I didn't anticipate how many visitors would inquire of the painting and whisper of murder and mayhem once they connected the beast to Henry."

My curiosity ignites. "Murder and mayhem?"

I've never thought to ask much about the history of the Addingtons. Many townsfolk have their opinions, and I ignore most of them. I recall someone mentioning a terrible tragedy involving a long-dead Addington relative and his two sons. At the time I figured it was an exaggerated tale, dramatized with each telling, but if the relative was the same man Selene painted as a beast, perhaps there may be some truth to said tale.

Selene smirks and brushes aside the matter. "It's not important. Just foolish whispers of betrayal and the consequences of a man overcome in a drunken rage."

I face her, turning my whole body toward her. "I believe I've heard the whispers, but are they true?"

Selene shakes her head and turns away from the painting. "I'll recall the horrid tale at a later time. I don't wish to ruin the excitement of my surprise. Come."

I follow, glancing at the painting one last time. "But can you at least confirm whether the rumors are true?"

My beloved Selene stops in her tracks and stares at the painting. "Would you think less of me if you knew Henry murdered his sons? Would your feelings change about my family if I acknowledged our connection to a murderer and how some believe we have inherited such a vile trait?"

In Linford there were many people with perilous pasts and shocking connections, and I never thought to hold the entire family responsible. The Addingtons surely have a few disgraces as well, but nothing could change how I feel about Selene.

"I believe I would think the opposite." I place my hand upon her shoulder, gradually sliding it to her hand. "It would only add to the mysteries of your family. All of you are so private and quiet. To discover a little scandalous excitement would be a welcomed change in pace."

Selene sighs and pulls her hand away. "I'm not sure if I'm delighted by your sentiment. Though, you would be the first to make light of the situation. Most people in Anna's Cove don't know what to believe, and because of their lack of knowledge, they fill in the blanks themselves. Some even go as far to claim that Henry murdered the very woman this town is named after."

I step closer to Selene, keeping my eyes upon hers. Her skin is smooth to my touch, softened by scented oils.

"There is nothing in this world that would make me think less of you. Not a single thing. You can keep your family's secrets. I'd prefer to live in the now and not allow the whispers of the past to shroud what joyous adventures await us." I try to smile, but I hear the hollowness in my words as Alfred's and Elara's voices echo the reminder of how Addingtons marry for money and not for love.

Glancing at the painting once last time, Selene sighs and kisses my cheek. "The image doesn't disturb you, even in the slightest?" she asks.

I choose to be brave. I don't want to upset her or hint how much the painting unnerves me.

"Not at all," I say, forcing a smile. "You're quite talented. I believe one day you'll have your portraits, landscapes, sketches, and fine doodles displayed in a gallery, and all who look upon them will think they are the finest ever created."

Her smile returns. "Assuming my future husband, whoever he may be, will approve of me earning a profit off my abilities. Most men in this society discourage my dreams. They blame my father for influencing me by diving into his profession without a second thought. The things people say regarding my aspirations—to them I say 'Foolery.' Someday, I'll walk through Linford City, parasol in hand, and see my work in the window of a fine gallery."

I want to insert my thoughts of support if ever I have the chance to wed her, but I bite my tongue instead.

"Never mind such foolish talk." Selene takes my hand and pulls me toward the far end of the room. "The adventure continues." Her grip tightens with excitement. "What I'm about to show you, you must promise to keep a secret. Keep it with your life, for if you tell anyone, I'll have to hunt you down and devour your soul. Do I make myself clear, Mr. Foster?"

Our eyes meet and I lean closer to her, detecting her sweet breath. Like children, we stand at the wall, crouched in suspense. "I swear it with every breath I take. I will never divulge whatever it is you wish to present. For upon doing so, may my soul be devoured by the only woman who brings such strange intrigue into my life."

We take a moment to laugh before Selene presses a hidden button within a wall plank.

I hear a click, and a section of the wall opens, revealing a secret walkway to an attic. Pulling me beside her, she leads me up a flight of steep, wooden steps to a large room.

"This used to be my grandfather's childhood bedroom. He shared it with all his siblings but made it private when he inherited the manor. It's one of the best hiding places Elara and I would use whenever we played hide-and-seek as children."

The large secret room is dusty and smells of must and mold. The walls are covered in gold and green wallpaper, and the floor is planked with polished wood. The ceiling comes to a point, forming an enormous triangle above double wooden doors leading outside to the roof. Besides two beds, the remaining furniture in the room is concealed by dust-covered sheets.

"Let's continue," Selene says, opening the wooden doors and motioning for me to follow.

Fresh air blows inside the room but doesn't relieve the musty stench.

"I take it this dusty room wasn't your surprise?" I motion to the place. "It's quite intriguing," I say, prompting a chuckle from my beloved.

Shaking her head, Selene escorts me through the doors to a small metal balcony. I stand, taking in a deep breath of fresh air, feeling the warm sun on my face. In the distance, there are miles of green rolling hills with patches of trees and poppy fields. To my right, as far as my sight can reach, is the seam where land meets sea. Anna's Cove is but a half-hour's walk to the water. Oh, how I wish my mother could have seen the waves and felt the sand between her toes. White puffy clouds drift across the sky, creating islands of faded shadows over the land.

"The view is remarkable," I say, appreciating the experience.

A satisfied chuckle escapes Selene before she makes her way down a metal ladder toward a plank of wood. Surrounded by slanted shingles on either side, Selene carefully makes her way along the plank, lifting her skirt past her ankles.

"Hurry," she says, giving me little time to make the descent.

My dearest Selene, always on some crazy adventure or discovery. I follow, carefully balancing myself along the plank until it ends at an inclined section of the roof. Several chimneys poke out among the shingled slopes, puffing out black smoke. Where we stand is almost dead center of the manor. The far edge, where the roof ends, is hidden from my view. Standing so high, I have no protection from a gusty wind that blows through my thick red hair and gives me a chill.

Selene is a few feet ahead of me, stepping lightly and balancing herself as if dancing on a highwire. "Are you coming?" she calls, her voice cheerful and light.

I take another deep breath and steady my wobbly legs. Have I mentioned I'm not too fond of heights?

I walk along another incline, my feet slipping on a few rotted shingles. I brace myself, trying not to snag my pants on jagged edges or dirty them in the gathered debris. I own three suits and can't afford another if I'm to accrue enough wealth to convince Mr. Addington to agree to my courtship with Selene.

She waits for me to catch up to her, her hands resting comfortably at her sides, her lips slightly parted. I can tell she's excited to have me here with her.

"Are you all right? Do be careful."

I puff out my chest and grin. "I'm quite fine. Scaling roofs is something I mastered while in my youth."

She detects my sarcasm, shakes her head, and chuckles. Carefully, she makes her way to the base of a nearby slope, holding folds of fabric in one hand to prevent tripping. I hesitantly follow, finding a small barrier at the base only a few feet away from the ledge. It's a small fence, perhaps a foot in height and decorated with spikes. I step gingerly over the barrier, the wind pressing against my body. Balancing, I glimpse the ground below and catch my breath.

I'm beginning to think this secret excursion is a little too adventurous for my liking.

"Selene, what exactly are we doing up here?" I ask, squeezing my eyes shut and leaning against the shingles at my side.

She's already a few feet ahead of me waiting patiently for me to join her. She shrugs and motions to an oak tree, large and almost encroaching on the manor. The trunk is perhaps five feet in diameter, and its limbs are so tangled and thick one can hardly see through its massive crown, even when the branches are bare in the winter.

Mr. Addington once mentioned how this particular tree was never to be cut down, for it represented the patience in growth. One can't become wealthy overnight; wealth must grow a little here, a little there, until it becomes as grand as this tree.

"Come and see." Selene breaks my thoughts and stretches out her hands, her smile widening as her excitement increases. "You must see the view."

I ignore the intimidating ledge as well as my tightening stomach. Balancing myself, I try to give Selene a brave look, but I can't. With sweaty palms and a stiffening body, I stop only a few steps away from my beloved darling.

"Fearful of heights, are you?" she asks.

"They aren't my favorite things to experience," I say, steadying my shaky voice and swallowing hard.

Selene is fearless. She pays no attention to the drop off in front of her. Instead she stares at the tree.

"As a child I leapt into the tree with my brothers."

When I lived in Linford I would swim in a nearby pond with my friends. We tied a rope to a branch and swung over the water. I gaze over the ledge once again and remind myself the difference between landing softly in pond water and hitting hard solid ground.

Selene extends her hand, her face filled with excitement. "Leap with me," she says.

CHAPTER 6

I'm not sure I hear her correctly. "What?" I ask. "Leap with you?"

I stare at the extended hand and laugh out loud. Does she honestly want to jump into the tree? The distance between the roof and the tree is too wide, in my opinion, and I don't think it wise. I wonder why she would ask such a foolish thing of me. Does she not understand how ridiculous this notion is?

"Devin," she says, her voice holding a serious tone. "Don't you trust me?"

I hesitate to acknowledge my lack of trust at the moment. I don't wish to offend her. My trust of Selene remains within the boundaries of my love for her. I trust she will never betray me. I trust she will defend my honor and uphold my standing as a man. I trust she will make any excuse on my behalf if we are caught at this moment, unescorted, by prying eyes. But I'm not sure I trust her with my life yet, let alone my livelihood.

If I were to fall and seriously injure myself, I would be no use to Mr. Addington. He'd probably terminate my apprenticeship due to my foolishness. Not to mention what the branches and twigs would do to my clothing. I only have two good suits for social gatherings, and I can't afford any rips and tears in this one. No . . . I cannot do what Selene is asking of me. I cannot trust her at this moment.

"I do trust you. But not in matters concerning childish things," I answer, thinking it will create the least offense. "We shouldn't stand so close to the ledge. If a gust of wind was strong enough, we could lose our footing and fall. We'd most certainly be injured."

Selene's smile momentarily fades, and she drops her hand. We stand in silence, her cheeks flushing with embarrassment. I try to think of words to justify my reasoning, but before I can speak my apology, she lets out a familiar laugh.

Whenever her mother disapproves of one of her wild ideas or socially unacceptable comments, Selene relieves the tension with her forced laughter. I recognize the downcast look, slumped shoulders, and pursed lips. She's speechless. She's disappointed.

Taking a final glimpse at the tree, she lets out a long sigh and forces a quick smile.

"Oh, you are quite right. I only wanted to cheer your spirits by sharing a bit of my cheerful childhood experiences." She motions to the tree once again. "The time we've spent together these past few months has prompted a renewal of hope and life within me. It's not often I come here anymore."

The feeling of disappointment strikes my heart and seeps into my veins. "I'm sorry, Selene. I've so much on my mind. I shouldn't even be here today, at the manor—"

"Then why did you come?"

Our eyes meet and I'm suddenly breathless. I don't know if I should answer truthfully or create another excuse.

Selene impatiently rolls her eyes. "It doesn't matter." She carefully makes her way to the metal balcony, climbing the nearest incline toward another flat surface much higher than before.

"I'm sorry I disappointed you. I'm not as adventurous as you wish," I say, retracing the path I took.

Selene stops at the base of the ladder, her arms folded tightly. "I'm not disappointed by your lack of adventure. I'm upset by your lack of trust."

"But what you're asking me to do is dangerous. I can't afford—"

"Had you trusted me, you would find I would never put you in greater danger than I think you could handle. You're brave enough to follow me toward the ledge, but apparently not brave enough to leap over it with me."

"Are you listening to yourself? What you're asking me to do is quite fatal, and I don't want to die. I've only begun my apprenticeship. With time I'll have my own clients, my own flow of wages. This is my chance to improve my financial status and finally be capable of providing for—" I mustn't say it. Not when she's this upset.

"For what?" Selene asks. "All men think about is money and power and control. Can we not live in a world that doesn't require such things? Even for a moment?"

My mind draws a blank. "I'm sorry."

But Selene is already climbing the ladder and returning inside the manor.

"Please stop," I call, climbing up once she's reached the balcony. "Please, Selene."

I enter the dusty room and take her by the hand. I don't want to leave things in such disarray. I want to explain my reason for avoiding the ledge and confess my feelings, hoping she will understand.

It's as if I'm standing on the ledge and feeling my heart flutter.

"What is it?" she implores. "What is it you want to say to me that you haven't already expressed?"

The words are on the tip of my tongue once again, but

something stops me from speaking.

Again she lets out a sigh of frustration and turns away. I don't want her to leave without knowing the feelings bursting from my heart.

"I love you, Selene, and I wish to spend the rest of my life by your side, if only you'll have me. My deepest desire is to bring you happiness. You inspire me to be greater than I am, to do more than I could ever imagine. You—"

"Stop, please," she says, holding her hands up. "Stop saying such foolish things."

My breath breaks from my throat. "But I love you," I say tenderly.

"Oh what do you even know about love?" She presses her fingers to her lips, regretting she spoke such words.

A silence fills the space between us. It thickens like the musty smell permeating the room. I know in my heart she didn't mean it. She's upset, offended by my reaction to her strange gesture of affection.

"I'm sorry," I say. "I suppose this isn't the best time to mention my feelings after all."

She composes herself, placing her hands at her sides. "No it isn't. It's a terrible time. I should be helping with the celebration."

I reach for her, but she steps away. I drop my hand. "Selene I couldn't let another moment pass without you knowing why I care so much about my apprenticeship and my potential wealth. It's my way to happiness with you." I try to take her hand again, but she remains distant. "Do you not at least share the same feelings for me?"

Fiddling with her fingers, Selene shakes her head and paces the floor as she chews her bottom lip. "This is all wrong. Why have you said such things? I thought we could remain in this dream a little longer. Remain within the foolish sentiments of secrecy and joy. In all honesty, who else have you ever loved? You speak of your mother's illness interrupting your life, keeping you from venturing into emotions, such as this, and when you come to Anna's Cove free to seek a courtship, I'm the first woman you meet."

Her face softens as she nibbles on her fingertips.

"I don't understand," I say, my voice catching in my throat. "What does it matter if I've had any experience with love? These past months spent in your presence have been wonderful. My most pressing concern is only to see you happy. The intimate conversations we've shared has opened my heart to put my trust in you. You do not judge me as others do. You do not see me as a poor man, nor do you speak to me as such. You give the humane respect I've rarely felt in my life. It would only be natural to turn our quiet love affair into an official courtship or engagement."

She stops pacing, wringing her hands tightly. "Nothing would please me more than to take upon your name. Though I once considered marriage a prison to which society expects me to surrender, I agree these past months have opened my heart again to love but . . ." She grows silent, her gaze piercing my heart.

I'm curious what thoughts race through her mind. It's as if she turned a switch, and her whole body relaxes almost instantly. Her face hardens and becomes void of all emotion.

"But you were just on your way out," she says, her tone now flat. "How silly of me to distract you from your exit. I will see you out."

She marches down the stairs, ignoring any notion of continuing our conversation.

I try to understand the sudden change in her demeanor. I've never seen Selene so distant. Clearly, I've spoken out of turn. Perhaps I've misunderstood all the times we've spent alone, the quiet moments sharing a tender embrace or gentle kiss. Am I wrong to think these actions were founded by affection?

I follow her through the recreation room, leaving the secret entrance wide open. Selene is determined to see me out the door, for she continues her march into the hallway, her shoes clacking with each step. I try to speak with her. She sweeps through the hall, guiding me toward the grand lobby.

"I'm sorry. I cannot continue visiting with you," she says with a stern tone. "I must help with the preparations for Marcus's engagement party this evening, and I'm sure there is some pressing matter you have to tend to as well."

The front door looms like gates leading to the dreaded dark abyss. I shouldn't make a scene—it isn't proper. Her silence upon the matter must be the result of shame over our secret dalliance, as one in her position could never sincerely love someone like me. I'm a man who must earn his wages to maintain food upon his table and clothes upon his back. How foolish was I to believe she would ever love me in the open for all to see?

"Ah, Selene, where have you been?" Mrs. Eliza Addington's voice echoes from upstairs.

Both Selene and I stand before the front door. Her mother motions for us to stop. Mrs. Addington lifts the front of her skirt and carefully walks down the stairs, meeting us on the main level of the grand lobby. The woman reminds me of a literal angel, pale complexion and golden blonde hair with even paler blue eyes. Smiling, Mrs. Addington places a hand upon her hip and fans herself with the other.

"I've been searching for you. I need help with the flower arrangements. I've sent Hattie to the kitchen and Deborah to the linens closet."

She searches for an expected escort, perhaps tucked discretely in the shadows but stops when she realizes the two of us are alone.

"Where's your escort?" she questions with one eyebrow lifted. "You know how improper it is to be unattended in the presence of a single young man. Should someone see you."

"Should someone see us? What are you talking about, Mother?" Selene replies, her face tight with anger.

My heart flutters, and I ball my hands into fists in order to keep them from trembling. Before Selene or I can explain, Elara steps out of the parlor, waving a book in the air.

"I found it. So sorry, Sister, for leaving you two alone for so long," she says loudly enough for everyone to hear.

Sighing with relief, I mirror Selene's face as Elara steps between us and lifts the book.

"I've been with them the whole time. We were just seeing Mr. Foster out, but I couldn't remember the passage in Theci's third sonnet. I simply had to find it, or my mind would have grown weary. And see . . . here it is."

She reads a silly passage of poetry about a dog and baby walking down a path toward a stream. It isn't the most impressive work, but it annoys Mrs. Addington enough to insist Elara stops reading.

"Mr. Foster," Mrs. Addington says, remembering something she'd long forgotten. "I believe I sent a last minute invitation in the post this morning officially inviting you to Marcus's engagement party tonight."

Selene and I exchange surprised looks. She tries to contain her bewilderment by pursing her lips tightly.

"I left before the post could arrive this morning," I say, my voice staggering. "I must have missed the invitation."

Mrs. Addington excuses Elara before looking me over. "Well, it doesn't matter now. Consider yourself invited and expected to attend. You are practically a friend of the family. It would only be fitting to have you among our guests tonight."

I hesitate to respond. She must see the perplexed look on my face, because she stands straight and stares at me like a beast watching its prey.

"As the matron of the family, I insist you come to the celebration tonight."

I force a smile, baring my teeth. "I appreciate the invitation, Mrs. Addington, and I will try to attend." It's a lie. I would be terribly uncomfortable among her esteemed guests.

Mrs. Addington's brow furrows, and she clenches the sides of her dress. "Mr. Foster, when a woman of the house invites you to a prestigious celebration, you do not turn her down, no matter the previous engagement."

Selene rolls her eyes. "Mother, don't be so demanding."

Mrs. Addington gives Selene a scolding look, quieting her daughter without a single word. "I am not being demanding," Mrs. Addington says, sternly, "but rather explaining how things are done here in Anna's Cove when properly invited by the lady of the house. Mr. Foster should know his place when it comes to social propriety."

Selene shrinks back, bowing her head respectfully. "My apologies. I was only going to convey my disappointment that he's far too busy to attend the celebration upon such short notice."

This prompts Mrs. Addington to look me over, her eyes narrowing along with her frown.

"Is this true? Are you too busy to attend one of the most important events in our family? It's not every day one of my children gets engaged to someone decent and proper. Have I told you Quintin is in town? He's bringing his dot of a wife." She takes a deep breath and relaxes her tight grip on her dress. "My apologies. I mustn't upset myself any longer. Please come tonight to join in the celebration. If anything, it will be good for your social status. I hear you are the subject of many conversations concerning your bachelorhood. Perhaps tonight you will be entreated by a possible future match."

Glancing at Selene and noting the disappointment on her face, I respectfully bow to Mrs. Addington. "I would be honored," I reluctantly say.

Mrs. Addington cups her hands over her heart. "Wonderful. There will be cake and wine and a ball. Are you familiar with the waltz?"

I'm not familiar with it whatsoever. I'm intimidated by the constant movement and knowing when and where to lead my partner.

"I am quite fond of it," I say confidently, adding but one more lie to my slew of deceits for the day.

"Wonderful," Selene practically shouts, her tone seething with frustration. "It's settled then. Mr. Foster will be in attendance tonight. Now I believe it's time for him to continue on with his day," Selene insists. She's practically pushing me toward the door.

"Excellent," Mrs. Addington says. "Be sure to wear a black suit and a white cravat. Festivities begin at seven o'clock sharp."

Turning away before I can say another word, Mrs. Addington calls for Selene to follow. I watch the older woman blend into the bustle of servants, leaving Selene and I alone once again.

My sweet dove finally opens the door, allowing me to step into the sun's light. "You honestly don't need to come if you don't wish it," she says, her voice still seething with disappointment.

"But I do wish it. Whatever I have said to withhold your reason for rejection, I hope I can convince you to express it, knowing my words are sincere. I have no intention of bringing you sadness or pain. And besides, offending your mother is the last thing I should do. Who knows what social repercussions may follow?"

I want her to smile, but she remains passive. "Good day," she says, remaining where she stands. "I hope you have an enjoyable evening."

I step further out the door, prompting Selene to slam it shut in my face.

"Good day, Miss Selene," I whisper. "Thank you for the lovely adventure."

CHAPTER 7

And she rejected you?" Harold asks, his face pinched with confusion. "Those Addington women are quite the mysteries, aren't they?" The man leans against the fireplace mantle, staring off into the ether.

I sit in the Taylors' quaint drawing room. A wall of windows and pink floral wallpaper serve as a backdrop to yellow furniture and a white fireplace. The mantle is topped with gold vases holding pink roses, freshly cut each day they're in bloom. Harold's Aunt Lydia rests in the far corner, soaking in the sun as she shivers with old age.

"This is all your fault," I say, wiggling in my chair at the memory of what transpired at the manor. "I shouldn't have listened to you."

I set the invitation down on a small table, contemplating putting it in the fireplace and lighting it ablaze. It's made of a thicker parchment with hand-drawn words and the family's signet stamped bottom-center of the page. The gaping wolf jaw

50

reminds me of Selene's painting.

I'm determined not to go tonight. Seeing Selene would only remind me of the day's horrible events. Since returning from Addington Manor, I've relived the moment I chastised her and the moment she rejected me. Remembering the disappointment and offense on her face makes my heart hurt. I should have trusted her. I should have set aside my foolish pride and at least stood at her side, seeing the world as she does. Instead I jumped to conclusions of madness, which is natural for my state of mind, but I should have handled the situation with more decorum.

"I'm not going, no matter what Mrs. Addington says," I finally erupt, folding my arms and resting my head against the side of the chair.

Harold breaks from his train of thought, walking to the invitation and looking it over. "No, you must go. It's bad luck to offend the mistress of the manor. Nothing good will come of it if you do not go."

I shrug off his words. "I don't care for old wives' tales. I have my freedom to choose, and if I choose to stay home tonight, then I choose to stay home tonight. Mrs. Addington doesn't own me. I'm not the Addingtons' slave."

Harold tucks the invitation into my jacket pocket. "Yes, and under any other circumstances I would hail your bravery and admire your self-proclamation of independence, but may I remind you how important it is to maintain a good relationship with your future mother-by-law? Eliza's opinion is as important as Arthur's and even if you managed to marry Selene without Eliza's blessing, you'd have to face her angry scowls for the rest of your existence."

He continues without taking a breath. "The mistress of the manor oversees all social interactions. She represents the family and must keep up positive appearances whether faced with scandal or compliments. You'll bring shame to the family if you reject her invitation and that shame extends to Arthur and you."

Harold paces the floor, motioning with his hands how

spectators would shield their mouths and whisper among one another. "Poor Mr. Addington. Finally extending an invitation to his apprentice, and the boy rejects it. Such an ungrateful boy. How could he do this to the man who took him off the streets?"

I tighten my arms around my chest and shake my head. Harold should become an actor for how exaggerated his motions are. Though I understand entirely what he's saying, my thoughts return to Selene and the dread of seeing her once again.

I know I cannot avoid her, because eventually I would have to return to Addington Manor for next week's work. But the thought of seeing her again only fills me with dread and regret.

"Why did Selene reject me?" I ask, shifting my weight in the comfy armchair. "None of our previous 'adventures' ever entailed a perilous journey to the roof. Was it some kind of test?"

Harold shrugs and strokes his unshaven chin. "It's rather romantic if you think about it. Just the two of you, away from prying eyes. I once tried to show Elara a particular grove of spring poppies. She chided me for separating us from Deborah and acting so scandalously. Had she ever taken me to that roof, I would have jumped. Yes, it would have been dangerous, but thrilling nonetheless."

I shake my head, wondering over the mental state of my only friend. There's no sign of liquor in the room, thank the Creator, so I know Harold is sober.

"If you think leaping off tall buildings is a romantic way of expressing one's love, you're madder than I thought."

Harold sits beside me, shrugging at the notion. "She's only bonding with you."

"Or driving me crazy."

We sit in silence, both interpreting Selene's strange actions. Harold appears hopeful, but I fear my thoughts have taken a turn for the worse.

"Why share so much affection and attention these past months, only to reject the thought of a future together?" I ask, still trying to understand her sudden change in demeaner.

"Perhaps she thinks me a toy to play with whenever she feels the need. Maybe she never loved me to begin with."

That must be it.

I stand and pace the large yellow rug, mulling over the possibility of Selene's feelings being disingenuous. It makes perfect sense. I remember watching the privileged people in Linford prance about with their secret lovers by night. It disgusted my mother, watching her closest friends associate with the wealthier men and being promised lives they would never live. Could Selene have inherited such a social trait?

Harold waves off the notion, resting deeper into his chair. "Selene is less reserved than Elara, but they both are fools when it comes to love. Selene simply chooses to express her love more freely. That doesn't mean it isn't real."

As I try to believe Harold, his aunt, Ms. Lydia Taylor, makes a disapproving sound and stamps her cane on the wooden floor.

"It's foolishness, all of it," she says. "Complete foolishness."

I view the frail woman dressed in black. Her grey-white hair is pulled tightly in a bun atop her head. Her weathered and wrinkled face clings to her skull as her faded green eyes hide behind clear spectacles. Her whole body shakes as if she's constantly being rocked on a turbulent lake.

"You be careful, Mr. Foster. The Addingtons are a cursed family. Only death follows them. I know it. I know it. Leaping off the roof was a test. I wouldn't be surprised if Miss Selene intended your demise. They are cursed. I know it. I surely know it."

Harold lets out a sigh and glances at his aunt. "Pay little attention to her. Her mind isn't as sharp as it once was!" he says, knowing she can hear him perfectly well.

She waves her cane at Harold and gives him a threatening growl. "Hold your tongue and remember, as I live and breathe, you are only given so much allowance to waste on your drink and women."

I try to maintain my respect by hiding my growing smile.

Ms. Taylor is always chastising Harold for his misbehavior. Harold claims she's ill, losing her mind and slowly growing frail each day. But by the looks of the woman, I think Harold has at least ten more years before Ms. Taylor finally shuffles off to the heavenly gates of the Creator's Hall.

"You shouldn't have come to Anna's Cove," Ms. Taylor continues, pointing her cane directly at me. "You shouldn't have accepted Mr. Addington's apprenticeship. There are other means of gaining one's wealth. My great ancestor, Phillis Holdenbrook, made a name for himself in crafting the sweetest wines. I still have a case of his first ten bottles. I told Harold to open one on my behalf when I'm finally in the ground."

"And such a day can't come any sooner," Harold adds, resting his head against the side of his armchair.

Ms. Taylor continues, her cane still held high. "Beware. Selene will be the death of you," she says. "They're cursed, connected to death. Do you understand? They're cursed, and you'll be cursed too."

I politely bow to the woman. "With all due respect, I don't understand what you mean by cursed. I've heard nothing but wonderful things about the Addingtons—"

"You're lying! You've heard the whispers about Henry and his vile and monstrous temper."

The thought of Selene's painting of Henry Addington flashes through my mind, validating the few rumors I've heard about a vicious drunk who murdered his sons. My smile fades, prompting the old woman to rest her cane. She pulls back her dry lips, sliding them off of her old wooden teeth.

"What you may have heard is only years of interpretation. The Addingtons are a cursed family. Death follows them everywhere they go. The Great Adversary is their proprietor, and forever they are indebted to him, offering fresh blood beneath the full moon whenever it is called for."

I listen attentively, leaning in as her voice lowers.

Even for a moment, Harold is silent.

"Do entreat me with the tale so I may learn the truth," I say, half sarcastic, half serious.

Ms. Taylor rests in her chair, the sun's light making her eyes almost translucent.

"What I am about to share will hopefully make you think twice about your affections for Selene Addington. I will tell you how it all began. I will tell the truth about the Addington's great ancestor, Henry William Addington."

Harold rolls his eyes. "Not this story again."

CHAPTER 8

I grab a wooden chair and sit comfortably beside Ms. Taylor. She leans on her cane, approving my attention and clears her raspy throat.

"Henry Addington was one of the first well-respected founders of Anna's Cove. Of course, this town wasn't originally called that. No, it was called Haven's Brook. But because of Henry's horrendous interactions, the name was later changed as a reminder to always respect the Addington family."

Harold lets out a loud sigh. "We don't need a history lesson. Get to the point."

Lydia growls once again, glowering at her nephew. "Don't interrupt. It's rude."

"Go on," I say. "Please."

Ms. Taylor places both hands now upon the cane and stares deep into my soul.

"Henry's eldest daughter, Fiona, returned home after spending the summer in Jared's Heath, near Linford. Henry was delighted to welcome her home, expecting to greet a well-refined woman ready for marriage to the local pastor. But much to his dismay, she was already engaged to a stranger named Richard Netter, whom she met at the boarding school for young women. Mr. Netter was a wash boy who seduced young Fiona with dreams of endless love, but Henry suspected the man was after Fiona's dowry."

Ms. Taylor grows tired of holding herself up and sets the cane upon her lap.

I remember visiting Jared's Heath once. The old boarding school for young women burned down before I was born, and a hospital stood in its place. I'd inquired about treatment for my mother's failing health, but we couldn't afford her staying there.

Lydia tilts her head, allowing more sun to splash over her thin skin. "Henry tried to humor his daughter, allowing Mr. Netter to remain at Addington Manor for a season, but he came to regret it. With the help of a foolish servant girl and a few falsified documents, Mr. Netter managed to steal over a third of the Addington wealth over the course of three months."

"Falsified documents?" I ask. "How?"

"Does it really matter?" Harold implores. "Tell him about the witch. You're wasting our time with all these theatrics."

Ms. Taylor's scowl deepens. "When Henry discovered this misfortune, he turned to the local witch for help. Within the shroud of nightfall, he went to Anna Onway, who lived in the woods not far from Addington Manor. It was she who listened to his plight and offered a solution to help kill the charlatan."

"Kill him? Isn't that a bit harsh? I would think throwing the fraud into prison would be more suitable," I say, not liking how extreme Henry was acting.

"Don't interrupt!" Ms. Taylor snaps. She searches her memory to where she left off. "Yes, Anna Onway offered Mr. Addington a potion giving him the strength of ten-thousand men, the speed of ten-thousand horses, and the ability to strike fear into the heart of anyone who looked upon him beneath the full moon's light."

"A man beast," I breathe, remembering the unnatural red eyes of Selene's painting.

"A man beast," Ms. Taylor repeats. "Yes, he was advised to drink the potion when the moon was at its brightest, but I don't think Henry took much thought to care what would happen to him once he did. He used his beloved Fiona to lure Mr. Netter to Addington Manor. She sent a letter to her estranged fiancé, offering more money if he returned to her in order to officially break off their engagement.

"Keep in mind, no official documents were signed in the first place, so they weren't engaged in the sight of society. But like a fool, Mr. Netter saw only the promised payment. He agreed to come, reaching an understanding to speak no word about the situation, thus keeping the Addington reputation intact and his pockets full."

Ms. Taylor's face grows grimmer, her eyes bulging as she leans closer to me. "Now, I confess, this part always chills my blood, so I warn you to be of good spirits." Her words prompt more groans from Harold. "Upon the night when the moon was at its fullest, Mr. Netter arrived at Addington Manor, but he never left.

"Accompanied by his two sons, Henry met with the young charlatan and waited for him to sign a simple parchment.

"Upon signing the parchment, Mr. Netter demanded his money, threatening if he wasn't paid in full, he would spread a rumor so vicious it would tear the Addingtons' good name to shreds. Instead of providing the agreed upon amount, his sons held Mr. Netter still as Henry drank the potion."

By this point I haven't blinked, and my eyes sting a little. "Did Henry transform?" I ask. I'm surprisingly invested in the story. Ms. Taylor has a profound way of engaging an audience.

"Yes," she says. "He became a vicious man beast, his body expanding and tearing through his clothes, the mounds of hair replacing his skin. The claws. The teeth. The unnatural red eyes."

"Just like Selene's painting," I say.

Ms. Taylor's eyebrows raise. "You've seen the painting? They actually have it on display?"

I nod. "Yes. Every time I frequent the recreation room, I feel the eyes staring at me."

Harold sits up from his chair, his forehead wrinkled above the nose. During his pursuit of Elara they would sit in the recreation room for a game of cards.

"Are you implying that horrible picture is, in fact, Henry Addington's personal portrait? It made me feel uneasy, unsettled," he says.

"And you have every right to feel so," Ms. Taylor says, wagging her finger at him. "Why Selene chose to paint such a horrid creature baffles me. Why remember the night where so much blood was spilt? Not only did Henry tear Mr. Netter limb from limb, but he killed both his sons, consuming their flesh and consummating the horrible family curse. When Henry awoke the next morning, he was found, naked and covered in blood, where the hedge maze now grows. With his embarrassment and disbelief, he searched for Anna Onway, blaming her for everything. He expressed the risk he now put his daughter and wife in, along with the rest of their children and servants. Anna denied the potion's power, telling him she gave him only pressed oil from flower petals and a few herbs."

"And do you believe her?" I ask.

"I think Anna lied and purposefully took revenge on the man who settled on her land, but I suppose it doesn't matter in the end. The following month, Henry transformed once again, slaughtering a few townsfolk. Enraged with himself, he promptly returned to the witch. Again, she denied everything and demanded he leave her alone. Between that day and the next full moon, Henry built a secret cellar away from the house, somewhere in the forest. He didn't wish to transform so close to the manor. Once that was finished, he needed to seek his revenge upon Anna.

"When the next full moon returned, Henry apologized to Anna and invited her to a family celebration as a way to make amends. As they made a toast to the engagement of Fiona and Parson Black, Henry weakened the witch."

Ms. Taylor places the tip of her cane upon the floor once again. "He drugged her, putting her into a deep sleep. I'm not exactly sure of the next few details—my memory isn't as sharp as it once was. But beneath the full moon, Henry transformed and murdered her."

The room goes silent as I think about the story. "What happened to the witch's body? If she had family, they would have tried to look for her."

Ms. Taylor shrugs. "Some say her body was dumped in the hidden cellar. Others claimed Henry ate every last bit of her in hopes it would break his curse. But regardless of what happened to the witch, it's what happened within the Addington family that remains a whisper spoken only in shadows."

Harold stands, motioning for his aunt to stop talking, but I stop him instead.

"What is this whisper you speak of?"

A faint smile stretches the wrinkles around her mouth. "Henry Addington vowed never to be swindled by anyone from that day forward, and he took it upon himself to decide who was worthy of the Addington name and association. Just as he culled his sheep, separating some for breeding and some for slaughter, he culled any possible suitor. Years passed until his two youngest children, Emilia and Sanford, were eligible for engagement. Sanford was the first to find himself a wealthy young lady, and Emilia was engaged to a gentleman two months later. Before either of them were married, the first official Culling was held. Luckily, both fiancés were spared but forced to keep the family secret or pay with their lives. Over the years, other suitors have met an unfortunate demise."

My stomach tightens as my thoughts linger on the beast feasting upon the innards of poor Mr. Netter and all the other possible suitors deemed unfit for the family name.

"How awful," I say, hiding my disgust.

"Yes, it is. Which is why you must leave the Addingtons alone at once. It is said Henry still stalks the land beneath the full moon. I've heard he's called upon by the eldest Addington male to prey upon unwanted suitors. Miss Selene might be the death of you after all."

CHAPTER 9

Harold calls for a nearby footman to help his aunt out of her chair. A young man enters and reaches the old woman's side.

"I think that's enough excitement for one afternoon," Harold says, assisting the footman with his aunt. Her chair creaks as they attempt to lift her.

The old woman protests, insisting both men let her go. They comply, and she plops back into her chair, growling at the two to leave her alone.

Harold throws his hands up and steps away. "You must get some rest. I'll have the servants serve your afternoon tea in bed, just as you like."

Ms. Taylor shakes her head. "Leave me be a little longer. I'm happy in the sunshine."

A pressing question wrings my mind, and I hesitate to ask, fearing the answer. Ms. Taylor sees how befuddled I am and motions for me to speak, shushing Harold at the same time. I'm afraid Harold will mock me, but I must know.

"If the Addingtons are connected to such a scandalous story, then why does anyone associate with them?" I ask, arguing with myself over the absurdity of the tale.

Chuckling, the old woman grips her cane and leans back in her chair. "Wealth, my dear man, is a precious tool when it comes to manipulating society to one's will. With how much wealth the Addingtons have accrued over the centuries from wise marriage matches, I dare say they could confess the validity of such a horrible story, and everyone would accept it with no questions. For if anyone speaks out of turn concerning the Addington family, they risk never being invited to another social gathering again. With how important it is to keep one's name fluttering on the wind, if you fall out of favor with an Addington, you might as well be dead."

But before I could continue my inquisition, Harold erupts into a great annoyance and steps between us.

"Enough with the drama," Harold chides. "Don't believe a word she says. It's the same story and ill advice she told me when I pursued Elara. There are no such things as man beasts. Henry Addington has been dead for centuries. You'll find his mausoleum in the Addington section of the cemetery. The story she told you is an obsessive exaggeration, cultivated by all those who are jealous of the Addington family because of their great wealth and social exclusion.

"Henry Addington was upset for being swindled, and he murdered a man in cold blood. That much is true. Like all unhappy, privileged men, he was unfaithful to his wife and had his mistress Anna killed as well. It is scandalous and embarrassing. Henry Addington was just as human as you or I. Now, please, don't allow this foolish woman to fill your impressionable mind with such folly."

I take offense of his description of my mind. I'm not impressionable. I'm open-minded when it comes to explaining the unexplainable. I'm quite grounded in logic but still have room for talk of supernatural or religious things. I'd like to believe the Creator exists and cares for all His creations, just as I believe the Adversary plays a devious part in tempting men to embrace the darkness they are naturally born with.

Clearly, Harold is upset. Maybe he mentioned the tale to Elara and was punished for it. He's never explained exactly why he couldn't continue to court Elara. Before her, he was a respectable man who honored propriety. I hope I remain the same honorable man, should Selene ever break off whatever secret arrangement we have—if she hasn't already.

"Be careful, Mr. Foster," Ms. Taylor says once again. "Stay home tonight. Though associating with the wealthiest family in Anna's Cove brings you many opportunities for growth in your own pursuits, the cost of your life isn't worth it. Don't be fooled, as Anna of old was. Don't fall prey to the Culling."

Harold ushers me out of the room. "We know, Aunt Lydia. We know. The family's cursed. Oooooooooooooh, beware."

I have a moment to bid the old woman a good day before Harold closes the door and walks me through the cottage.

"Pay no attention to her. She's mad. It's her way of being vicious toward the Addingtons."

"But how does she know such a story to begin with?"

Harold places a heavy hand upon my shoulder. "Before Mr. Brent became the Addingtons' butler, he was a stable hand. Aunt Lydia was friends with Mr. Addington's Aunt Demora. Lydia developed feelings for Mr. Brent and supposedly had her own excitable affair with him. I'm sure gossip spread among the servants, exciting such a tale."

To imagine Mr. Brent young and reckless gives me pause.

"And to imagine, Jamison Brent might have been your uncle," I say, fighting the urge to chuckle.

Harold ignores me. "Thank the Creator, she settled into society as an heiress to the family winery. Which reminds me, Mrs. Addington ordered ten cases of wine and personally invited me as a means of thanks for my family's contribution."

We make our way down the stairs to the main level of the cottage. The sun shines brightly through the drawn curtains, filling the rooms with a warm light. The cottage is cozy and filled with marble statues of animals. I suppose Ms. Taylor is a lover of foxes, for she displays many of them all throughout her residence.

"I wonder why Jamison would tell such a tale when he holds the family with such high regard?" I ask, stopping at the base of the stairs.

Shrugging, Harold sighs and reaches for the door. "Perhaps he was a foolish young man who wanted to impress a beautiful girl. Men do strange things when it comes to love."

I laugh at the notion. "Yes, like risk their livelihood all for a roll in the shade. This day has already gone terribly wrong. I'm not going tonight."

"But you must. Mr. James Blueshire intends me to court his sister, Penny, and has invited me to ride with them. I'm not interested in the slightest, but I had no excuse to decline without offending Mr. Blueshire. Please don't give him the opportunity to leave me alone with that pitiful woman."

We step outside, shielding our eyes until they adjust to the brightness of the sun. Our boots clomp through the gravel drive leading away from Taylor Cottage.

"But Elara will be there," I remind him, hoping it will deter him from his insistence.

"Another reason you must join me, as her fiancé will be at her side the entire evening."

Harold makes exaggerated motions, mimicking Mr. Bottrell's mannerisms. He snorts like a pig before rolling his eyes. "But I am a man of strong character and will not allow my travails to keep me from drinking and dancing."

I stare at the man, curious about his encouragement of my intentions with Selene. "Why do you persist so much? I get a strange feeling this has more to do with Elara than avoiding Penny."

He brushes aside the notion, places his hands upon his waist, and scoffs. He wants to avoid the conversation, but something changes his mind, and he releases a long exhale. "The very thought of Elara incites an overwhelming feeling of torture. I was convinced she loved me. I was determined to court her, thinking it was what we both wanted. But like blowing out a candle, her interest in me suddenly stopped. I begged for a reason, but she remained silent. And three months later she's engaged." He chuckles to lighten the tension. "Maybe there's some truth to my aunt's silly tale, and Elara has preserved me from facing disembowelment at a Culling," he says jokingly.

He paces a little, turning his attention to anything but me. His face softens back into the hazy look he gets whenever Elara crosses his mind.

"So if you'll forgive my insistence and encouragement of you and Selene," he says, his tone softening with each step he takes, "I think it best at least one of us finds joy in love with an Addington daughter. Besides, you're a dear friend and good man. There's a calm innocence about you, and you know the name of every servant at Addington Manor. I can't even tell which footman is Jared and who is Aaron."

I smile at the compliment. I'm grateful he explains himself. I always worry about Harold and his darker moments filled with self-loathing and alcohol. It's nice to see his more sentimental side.

But such sentiments only last a few moments before he claps my back and laughs, "So despite my failure to figure out the truth behind Elara's erratic behavior, you must persevere in discovering the reason behind Selene's rejection. Tonight's your opportunity."

"But what if something terrible happens?" I ask.

We near the wooden gate leading to the road. Leaning against the splintered slates, Harold crosses his arms. "Like what? The slaughter of Marcus's intended bride?"

I'm quiet, prompting him to roll his eyes and sigh deeply.

"Gracious man, nothing terrible will happen, though there's no objection to Mr. Bottrell's demise," he says, before breaking into his usual habit of describing how flawlessly the evening will go. "You and I will arrive closer to eight—"

"But it starts at seven."

"Yes, but reasonable men arrive fashionably late. We'll allow the women to fawn over our absence, worry a little and wonder if we're coming at all. And when we do arrive, you'll search out Selene, get right to bottom of it all, demanding she explain herself."

Of course, I'm not one to demand anything of anyone, but how Harold explains the plan excites a little confidence within me.

"And what will you be doing?" I ask, giving him a sly look.

I know he wouldn't bother with Elara. She's engaged and cannot be spoken to unless she begins the conversation. Judging by how cold the young woman can be, I suspect she'll keep her lips sealed if Harold tries to catch her attention.

Harold mimics my sly look, his cheeks flushing a slight pink. "I'll be doing what I do best, my dearest friend. Drinking and dancing with the most beautiful daughters in all of Anna's Cove."

We share a good laugh, and I step through the gate, catching the scent of poppies on the breeze.

"I'll pick you up around eight o'clock. Remember your black suit and white cravat. It's what all upper privileged men wear when flaunting their wealth," Harold says with a smile.

"I have no wealth to my name," I say, reminding myself more than Harold.

He pulls a twig from a nearby tree and whips it about. "But if you're successful in charming Selene tonight, perhaps months from now you will have more wealth than you could ever imagine. And it won't matter what foolish tales or unnecessary *whispers* are spoken about the Addingtons. You'll be connected to them, and that's everything anyone in this wretched little town desires."

I can hear a little resentment in his tone. A tinge of regret in his eyes.

"I suppose I'm convinced. Thank you, Harold. I'll await your carriage this evening."

He waves me goodbye. I walk away from Taylor Cottage, still filled with worry about tonight.

CHAPTER 10

I arrive promptly at eight o'clock accompanied by Harold, Miss Penny Blueshire, and her brother James. The Blueshires manufacture all the candles in Anna's Cove, making them a well-respected family among the privileged. Like most women in town, Penny has tried to get Harold's attention and assumes riding with us to the celebration will somehow single her out. I pity the girl. He hasn't spoken a word to her nor made any eye contact, making his disinterest quite clear.

"I find it rather funny how Mrs. Addington only invited the families who provided supplies for this celebration," Mr. Blueshire says as the carriage passes the well-lit pond. Several torches line the drive, directing the coach drivers straight to the front door and then to the stables around back. "Those are Mr. Hatchet's torches, and he's mentioned his invitation."

Penny snorts as she chuckles at the comment. "It's her way of supporting everyone in town. Harold's aunt provided the wine, we provided the candles and—" The red headed woman pauses, glancing at me. "And what do you provide Mr. Foster?"

I think for a moment, an awkward silence fills the carriage.

"Company," Harold interrupts. "He provides company, Miss Blueshire."

She blushes. It's the first moment of attention Harold's given her.

Harold continues. "I hope you discover the same while chittering with your dear friends."

Penny's face darkens as Harold's intention to avoid her is understood..

The carriage comes to a halt, and footmen escort us to the front door. The scent of lavender fills the air, wafting from flowering bushes lining the grounds. Everything is bathed in a filter of white from the bright, full moon rising above the horizon. Not a cloud in sight.

"A full moon's out tonight," Harold says, laughing as he mimics his aunt. "Beware of the Addington curse."

I scowl at his glib remark. "Don't say such things."

"Or what? Henry will jump out from the shadows and tear me limb from limb? Aunt Lydia's rubbish story is fool's folly and nothing but a whisper upon the wind. You remember what we planned?"

I nod, laughing at his childishness.

"Good. And good luck. May we both end this evening with a smiles upon our faces."

Harold walks around Penny, who's waiting for him to escort her inside, and marches into Addington Manor, playfully nodding to the footman at the door.

The others enter, but I wait a moment. My stomach is tied with a thousand knots, and I'm already beginning to sweat beneath my collar. The footman politely waits for me to enter, keeping quiet as I step up to the door, only to return to the gravel.

I can do this. Harold is right; I must know the truth.

I'm sure I appear crazy, hesitating to enter.

My mind has been reeling all day about what I would do

and what I would say to Selene. Clearly, I'm going mad.

I take a moment to clear my mind and settle myself. Once ready, I enter, stepping confidently onto the polished tile and into the fray of high-social company.

The grand lobby is filled with people admiring every little detail of the manor. All the women are dressed in light pink and yellow, large feathers in their hair, while the men wear the fanciest black suits and buttoned shoes. I watch Harold already socializing with a group of people in the parlor, the sound of piano music filling the small room as old men puff their cigars and drink glasses of wine.

I carefully make my way to a large book and sign my name with a feather quill.

"Welcome, Mr. Foster," the man says, recognizing me.

"Charles," I say with a half nod.

"Come, dear friend. The night is young," Harold says, startling me. The scent of cigar smoke lingers on his suit, and already he holds a cup of wine.

He pulls me away from the lobby and into the ballroom.

Three golden chandeliers hang from a low ceiling and create a heavenly glow accompanying the lit candles placed upon golden sconces throughout the room. I recall a few servants grumbling yesterday at how difficult it was to dust every cup by hand and replace every candle.

A large band of strings and woodwinds plays in the far corner, filling the air with a jovial tune. Round tables line the far wall of windows. The long red curtains are pulled back, allowing the bright moon's light to stream inside. I recall Ms. Taylor's story about Anna's last night alive. Could the celebration have been as extravagant as this?

At the center of the room is a concord of dancers, each cheerfully bowing and turning, walking and clapping. Their rhythmic movements break up the groups of people standing and chatting about their blissful days or latest gossip.

And among all the guests and beautiful bustle are several

members of the well-mannered Addington family. Both relief and disappointment wash over me when I discover Selene isn't among them.

They are dressed in shades of red, Elara wearing the darkest. Both Marcus and his brother Quintin wear pressed velvet suits accented with red cravats around their necks. Marcus stands with his fiancée, Diane Kendall, near a long table in the back of the room. They are surrounded by plates of pastries and bottles of wine.

The Kendalls provide no product to Anna's Cove. They've attained their wealth through marriage and inheritance.

The handsome couple welcomes the many congratulations and greets each guest with a smile. Diane stands out the most in a pure white dress hemmed with crimson embroidered doves lined with shiny beads. Her blonde curls are accented with red roses, and she has tied a matching choker at her neck. She looks at Marcus as she sips her red wine, her blue eyes reflecting his smile and tender looks.

Looking around the room for Selene, I fail to find her. Instead, I observe the newly returned Quintin and his wife, Sophia. Unlike the family she's married into, she wears a navy blue dress. Her black hair is pulled tightly into a bun. The beautiful woman isn't smiling, though, and she stands closer to her husband, avoiding eye contact with those around them. I don't blame her for her bashfulness. It's as if she's on display for all to see and marvel upon. Sophia isn't like most women in Anna's Cove, who would feel honored for the attention.

I move toward the center of the room and notice the various spectators leaning to stare at Sophia. I wonder at their behavior toward a colored person, as if they've never seen a darker race before. In Linford there are many people of different races among both the rich and the poor, and they aren't treated differently. It's not like colored people don't exist in Anna's Cove, but clearly, they aren't recognized or remembered.

"Quintin has brought home a delightful addition to the

family," a woman says beside me. I turn to reply, believing she's addressing me, but find she's speaking to Eliza Addington.

"Alas, I fear Quintin intends to annul his relationship as soon as possible," Eliza says. "Seeing her among his siblings has convinced him he's made a mistake."

She opens her red lace fan and hides her mouth behind it. She and Mrs. Kensy, the pastor's wife, fan themselves as they consider the gossip.

"I wanted to welcome Sophia with open arms, but I fear she's only here to take advantage of my son and steal away his money," Eliza says in a high pitched voice. "I am saddened by the assumption, but she claims no wealth or title. I do love her dark skin. Reminds me of rich chocolate." She sighs. "Such beauty is wasted on a girl with no prospects. Their children would have looked pleasant in pastel."

Mrs. Kensy hides her expression behind a white lace fan. She always strives to flatter the women she wishes to impress, and she's doubtless seeking to make the most of this time she has Mrs. Addington to herself. She lowers her fan and says, "You have such a large heart. Doing your best to accept your son's unfortunate marriage. Such charity. What a blessing it is to have him home again. These past five years must have been dreadful for you."

Eliza nods, forcing a sympathetic smile.

"I pray the Creator blesses your family in the weeks to come," Mrs. Kensy says, wrinkling her forehead as she pouts. "I hope you settle this chaotic affair with Quintin and his heathen wife. Do you know if she worships the Creator? I'm not too familiar with the religious stance in Delova. I hear they worship nature more than anything."

"She isn't a believer. It is sad. I might have been able to overlook her poverty and heathenistic ways, had Quintin courted her properly and with our blessing. I don't like surprises, and Sophia is filled with them. I appreciate your prayers, and I believe Quintin's situation will be resolved soon enough."

I don't realize it at first, but my hands are pressed into tight fists. Eliza Addington speaks lies. I don't care what Harold says about seeking her approval. If I win Selene's hand in marriage, I'd rather ignore her evil looks than pretend to be agreeable to the intolerance and pure evil that spills from Eliza's lips.

I follow Eliza's glare toward the women surrounding Sophia and finally see Selene as she joins her family. Her dress mimics the color of candlelight shining through red wine, she's always a vision, no matter what color she wears. I catch myself staring and turn away from her to collect myself.

Elara stands near Selene, doing her best to smile and socialize, but she's clearly distracted. Her fiancé is nowhere to be seen.

I start my journey around the line of dancers, their hops shaking the floor as they form two lines and circle one another. The scent of sweat and perfume mixes, and the air thickens. I keep a good eye upon my beloved. She laughs at something Quintin says, and I can hear his deep voice explaining the sound of fallen trees. I don't wish to interrupt the conversation, so I keep my distance, turning out of sight the moment Selene looks in my direction.

"You make Delova sound like a dream," Selene says to her brother.

"Because it is. Miles of forest. The air is fresh and filled with the scent of pine. You should visit us, both you and Elara," Quintin says, kissing Sophia's hand as he tries to relieve the troubled look on her face.

Elara smirks. "It sounds lovely, but Keagan intends to live on the mainland for our first year of marriage. I fear visiting Delova will have to wait."

Quintin respectfully bows to his sister and unbuttons his jacket. "I understand." He claps his meaty hands together, unbuttons his vest, and loosens his cravat. "Dear ladies, I am parched, and the air is rather suffocating. If you will excuse me, I must taste the latest vintage of the Taylor wine. I hear it's delightful."

I watch Quintin turn from his sisters and wife, his dark eyes cautiously looking over the room as he walks toward the serving table. Harold greets Quintin as he passes and asks about Delova. He catches Elara's attention, and a glum exchange occurs between the two.

I inch my way closer to the women, hoping to ask Selene to dance, but I'm too late.

Mr. Blueshire politely takes Selene's hand and leads her across the room.

The band begins a waltz, and I watch as she laughs and moves about in the arms of another man. A part of me imagines her happier with somebody else. Perhaps I truly should accept her rejection and stop fooling myself.

"Mr. Foster," Elara says with a devious smile. "Welcome."

I have no desire to carry on a conversation, fearing Elara will try to remind me of my place in society.

"Hello, Miss Elara. My apologies. I must excuse myself," I say, turning away from her and Sophia as soon as I can.

I backtrack my steps, loosening my white cravat, sweat beading on my forehead. So many people are now crowded into the ballroom, making it difficult for me to leave. I push my way against the stream of guests, finally breaking free but feeling no relief. The grand lobby is still packed.

Instead of making my way out of the manor, I inch my way across the grand hallway to the gallery door. Opening it, I find the room empty and dark. Only the moon's light radiates in the far corner, encouraging me to walk toward it.

It's quiet here, and the air is much cooler. The room is filled with family portraits and other fancy paintings, statues, busts, and expensive vases. Once at the window, I try to open it to get some fresh air, but I can't. At the windowsill, three nails are covered with white paint, securing the window shut.

How odd.

Finding no relief, I remove my cravat entirely and dab my

sweaty forehead and neck. I step away from the window, almost tripping on a wrinkle in the rug.

A thin line of flickering light catches my attention, and I pull away the rug, revealing a secret door.

Arthur allowed Marcus to dabble with stonemasonry and gave him permission to build an additional cellar for food storage, but I thought it was closer to the kitchen. Curiosity overcomes me, and I desire to see his handy work. I carefully lift the small, black ring attached to the cellar door. Music swells from the ballroom, reminding me of Selene dancing with Mr. Blueshire. I'd prefer to investigate this strange little place.

Flickering candlelight reveals smooth stone steps and a narrow entryway. I step inside, lowering the door.

CHAPTER 11

I plant my feet at the base of the cellar, admiring the craftmanship of the smooth stones. A large, thick candle burns within a stone alcove, its dim light dancing about, mixing shadow and light on the stone walls. The cellar smells of mortar, damp cement, and candle wax. I'm not sure why the candle is burning unattended, and I'm half tempted to blow it out before I leave.

A few steps from where I stand, the cellar opens wider, but there are no shelves for storage. I see no sacks of grain, bottles of fruit, or cured meats or cheeses. In fact, the cellar is completely empty. The walls are bare and painted white. I search the small space. It's tall enough for me to stand upright, and I smirk at the thought of any of the Addington men walking around hunched over. To my left, the cellar deepens to a space wide enough for two adults to stand side by side. Shiny metal bars reflect the candle's light.

It looks as though Marcus has constructed a prison. Could this be an extension to the gallery? Maybe it's a form of living art.

I step closer to the separated space and see no lock or key. Instead, I observe a strange contraption attached to the barred door. There are metal buttons and indents, indicating it's a specialized lock. I saw a few of these at the Oxlin Bank when Arthur introduced me to the man we report our financial information to. The lock requires a specific combination of twists and turns or pushing buttons. Judging by the brightness of the metal, similar to the thick bars, I suspect it's made of silver or steel.

Why would Marcus create such a place? And why is the candle burning with no one around? The cellar doesn't feel right to me, and I turn to leave.

Footsteps just outside the cellar door force me to freeze midstride. I hold my breath, praying I won't be discovered.

"Are you prepared for this evening?" a man's voice speaks.

At first, it's muffled and distant. I tiptoe closer to the stairs, carefully climbing until I must sit, my ear pressed against the wood.

"I've been informed of the changes and what is to be expected," another man speaks. The voice is deep, the tone assertive. "But I don't understand why things have changed."

The first man chuckles. "My brother once expressed how our traditions were harming our family rather than strengthening it. I fear his emotions have drawn him further away from what we Addingtons represent, and I wish to prove his progressive ideals wrong. These changes are meant to prove a point."

There's a moment of silence between the men. I now recognize one of the men to be Alfred.

"And you think he'll agree with our arrangement?" the other man asks.

I listen attentively, my body stiff as I sit upon the stone steps.

"I believe he'll have no choice after tonight. The price you're willing to pay is something I believe no father can turn down. I imagine it would cover the first five years of marriage with no question. Come. We will find my brother and bring him here to explain why you are the rightful suitor for Selene."

My heart races at the mention of Selene.

I shift my weight on the stone step and clench my fists. Is this truly happening? Alfred can't present a suitor, as Arthur oversees selecting a mate for his daughters. I remember this morning, standing outside the study listening to Alfred's distaste of his brother's newfound decisions. Could the suitor have been mentioned? I sensed Alfred's displeasure of me. He obviously suspects my feelings for Selene, and perhaps this inspired him to present an alternative before Arthur and put a stop to any possibility of my courting Selene.

In a moment of rage, I bump my head on the cellar door, lifting it a little.

"What was that?" the second man questions.

I freeze. If they find me here—

Alfred clears his throat. "Never mind. It came from the hallway. It's time to set things into motion. I cannot have my brother continue disgracing the family name. Your offer will outweigh any chance of another suitor taking claim of Selene. After tonight, you will have full association with the Addingtons—I guarantee it."

"Thank you, Alfred. I'll do my best to not disappoint you. I have always admired the Addington way and will strive to uphold the family's traditions until my last breath."

"I know, dear man, I know. You will only bring greater power and status to us once our families are unified."

I listen carefully as the two leave the gallery, closing the door behind them. My eyes drift to the candlelight dancing against the stone floor. If what Alfred says is true about the amount the suitor is willing to pay, then I stand no chance in making an offer to Arthur in regards of Selene's hand in marriage.

My first instinct is to accept the fact I have no chance, nor have I ever, to marry Selene. All my life I've accepted things the way they are. I have no luxury or freedom to do as I please. If I wasn't working for my next meal or saving what trinkets I could to sell, I was helping my mother survive, keeping us out of the poorhouses. Unfortunately, my first taste of freedom was when my mother took her last breath, begging me to do better, to be better.

But the better life I'm striving for is still out of reach. I'm in the right direction but have quite a ways to go.

And yet, despite my lack of confidence, I'm emboldened with a sense of hope that I'm not too late to achieve what I desire.

I love Selene, and, in spite of her puzzling behavior today, I believe she loves me. If only she could freely proclaim it, we could then go to her father and appeal to his kind nature. I know it would take time to save enough money to properly support her, but I can hope Arthur would be patient and understanding.

Selene and I are a good match. We bring out the best in each other. I would support and encourage her outspokenness, feeling it an honor to have such a confident and talented wife. I know she isn't a prize to be won or bought, but a companion to venture through life with. I love her. I love her wit and charm, her beauty, and how she inspires me to be a better man. I cannot go another moment wondering if she sincerely loves me or not. I cannot waste any more time wallowing.

I must know how she feels and assure her that we can find a way through the obstacles which keep her from loving me fully. It's unlikely I'll succeed, given the deeply rooted social customs of Anna's Cove, but I think Harold's influence is finally affecting me for the worse.

I make my resolve, determined to march straight to Selene and speak with her.

I carefully lift the cellar door, my gaze searching the empty room before leaving the stairs. Replacing things as they were before, I make my exit out of the gallery only to be stopped by Quintin Addington.

"My apologies," he says, pausing when he recognizes my face. "Mr. Foster, is it? I never had a chance to express how grateful I am my father has taken on a hobby to help someone less fortunate." He takes my hand, shaking it firmly and smiling.

It seems Quintin has taken on a few social greetings from Delova, where they use a handshake instead of a polite nod or deep bow. I hear such formalities aren't as important there, thus the assumption that those from Delova are uncivilized compared to the rest of the occupants on Mina Island.

Quintin dabs his forehead with his loose cravat. He unbuttons the top of his shirt, rubbing his neck with his fingers.

"It's quite the hobby indeed," I say, hiding my offense. "How are you liking being home after such a long absence?"

He tucks his cravat into a deep pocket of his red velvet jacket. "Take no offense, but I care for nothing connected to this place. I only traveled here upon Sophia's request. She wished to understand more about my family and, like a fool madly in love, I acquiesced."

Quintin glances around the many guests wandering the hall and lobby. He reminds me of a trapped animal searching for a way out. I'm impressed by his eloquence.

"Are you all right? You seem uncomfortable," I say.

He runs a hand through his dark brown hair and flashes a half smile. "I'm actually on my way out for a bit of fresh air. I'm not used to so many people in one place," he says, looking over the guests wandering about the grand lobby. "None of our social gatherings in Harlic quite match this spectacle. But I digress. It was a pleasure to speak with you. I've heard many great things about you from my father. But if you'll excuse me now, I must leave if I'm to return in time for my father to present the Grand Toast to Marcus."

He politely nods before weaving his way through guests who barely recognize him. I watch attentively as he vanishes out the front door, brushing aside the footman's greeting.

Laughter from the ballroom reminds me of my determined mission. I enter the room once again, searching for Selene, finding my beloved dancing with a stranger and smiling. In the peaceful glow of candlelight she's radiant, attracting the gaze of all surrounding men.

Am I a fool to be so persistent?

I grab a chalice from the nearest serving tray and drink the red contents quickly, feeling the alcohol bubble to my stomach. I must be assertive but not overbearing. The lively gavotte energizes the room as dancers raise their hands and walk around one another. Selene links hands with her partner, and they take their turn skipping through a tunnel created by the others.

I remain focused, pacing my steps as the song draws to an end. The final measures ring through the air, prompting everyone to clap and cheer. I take advantage of this lull between songs.

Without hesitation I step directly to Selene and call her name. She stops, recognizing my voice, and takes her time facing me. When our eyes meet, she fiddles with her fingers, stroking the red chocker around her neck.

"Mr. Foster," she says.

I extend my hand palm up, memorizing her beautiful face. "Miss Selene, would you give me the pleasure of this next dance?" I ask gently.

I'd rather escort her from the room to speak, but that would draw greater attention from prying eyes. At least while dancing, any suspicion of us would be unfounded.

At first her eyes skim over those surrounding us. I fear she's going to reject me once again, but then Selene places her hand in mine and nods slowly.

"The pleasure would be all mine," she says with a soft smile.

We make our way toward the center of the room as the music begins. It's a waltz, a form of dance I'm not too familiar with, but I know enough to place my hand between her shoulder blades and make a soft fist. Her brown eyes remain focused on me as she flashes a coy smile. My heart races as I bring her closer, and I find it difficult to think about anything else at the moment. We follow the flow of dancers and circle the floor in a sea of pastels, feathers, and black jackets.

"I thought you didn't know how to waltz," Selene says.

I turn her slightly to the right, avoiding another couple whose elbows are extended too high. "I suppose now is as good of a time as ever to practice, though I'm not necessarily comfortable with the footwork."

I twirl her, coaxing a giggle. She returns to me, her dress swishing as we step in rhythm.

"And may I ask what has inspired you to broaden your horizons?" she says, keeping a serious eye upon me as we dance.

We glide across the floor, my hand directing her as we keep our eyes connected. "I have realized how frightened I've been to truly live. This realization came to me after I spoke out of turn and offended the kind heart of a dear friend. I only wanted her to know how my fondest feelings have grown over these few months, but I regrettably took no consideration of how problematic it could be for her to know what is in my heart. I'm a man of humble means, and though I may not have much experience in romantic love, I know what true love entails. Whatever I may lack when it comes to the affairs of the heart, I'm willing to learn if she's willing to teach me."

Selene crinkles her nose a bit. "You have quite the way with words. Perhaps you should become a poet instead of an accountant."

We share a chuckle at the thought before she continues to speak. "I'm sure your beloved friend recognizes what kind of man you are and would admit she acted inconsiderately of your feelings. Her assumption that the two of you were merely sharing an adventure was truly childish. It was wrong of me to speak—"

She pauses, staring deeply at me, and biting her bottom lip.

"Speak?" I ask. "You did no wrong by stating the obvious. I may be foolish to love you, knowing I could not provide what you deserve, but to chastise you for sharing something of great value and importance was wrong of me."

She shakes her head. "No. Nothing was wrong with what you did, with the exception of refusing to see the view by my side. We wouldn't have had to leap, though I still think it would have been invigorating."

"I'm sure it would have been. And I promise to return there to see it once again with you if you wish."

We move with a group of dancers twirling around us in swirls of color.

She smiles, tightening her grasp upon my hand. "I do wish it. I'm sorry I turned away so coldly from you, but I do beg your patience in replying to your proposal."

"I only need to know why you rejected me in the first place. Everything else can wait."

She feels lighter in my arms, everything about her is lighter. Can this be the moment she explains herself? She opens her mouth to speak. She appears confident in what she'll say, speaking the words I have waited to hear. But as she begins to suggest we duck away for more privacy, something distracts her from beyond my shoulder.

"What is he doing here?" she asks. Without any explanation, she leaves my side, moving through the swirling crowd of dancers and toward the front of the room.

I follow after her, traveling against the direction of the dancers, dodging men and women turning about as they shift their paths to avoid me.

I watch Selene march toward a man dressed in black. She's animated, using wide gestures with her arms.

Elara steps in front of me, her mouth contorted into a half smile.

"Just when I thought this night couldn't get any worse, Mr. Rothbottom appears out of nowhere. Do let me know when Sophia finally cries. I'll be distracted with Selene."

Elara waves toward the dark beauty staring out of a window, her bottom lip trembling. Wishing something could be done to comfort her, my heart softens when Diane approaches Sophia and begins a conversation.

Elara huffs at the turn of events. "Never mind." She sips her wine and returns her attention to Selene.

"Who is Mr. Rothbottom?" I ask, though I don't want to know the answer.

Her smile widens, and I wait for a forked tongue to slither between her lips. "He's Selene's fiancé."

CHAPTER 12

Glaring at Elara, I pray she's trying to get a reaction out of me. I swear the woman delights in making me suffer. I wish I could say her contemptuous treatment toward me is a sign of a disingenuous heart torn between desires and expectations, but she's been ill-tempered since the day I met her.

"Fiancé?" I repeat. The word leaves a bad taste in my mouth.

Her dark eyes scan the room, and she sets her half-empty glass upon a nearby serving tray.

"This obviously isn't the place to discuss such personal matters. If you wish to truly know—"

"I do wish to know. Who is this stranger upsetting Selene? She never mentioned a fiancé. I would think such a detail would be one of the first topics of discussion."

Holding up a hand to silence me, Elara breaks eye contact while speaking. "I'm going to leave this room shortly, and once I'm through the door, I'll need you to slowly count to ten and meet me in the drawing room."

I scan the room and I don't see any prying eyes glancing in our direction. Hardly anyone pays attention to Elara since she became engaged.

"All right. The drawing room," I say, my stomach aching as if filled with rocks.

Elara promptly excuses herself, moving through the crowd in a swift manner, and escapes the ballroom without saying a word to anyone.

Ten . . . Nine . . .

Selene still speaks with Mr. Rothbottom, her face knitted with tension. I wish I could hear what they're discussing, but they stand too close and speak too low. Though Selene's rigid posture and straight back suggests she isn't happy with the stranger, Mr. Rothbottom appears relaxed and calm. The small distance between their bodies fills me with a desire to march over and step in between.

Eight . . . Seven . . .

I wonder why Selene never mentioned Mr. Rothbottom. If he truly is her fiancé, then I'm ashamed and embarrassed to be played by Selene's playful wiles. And yet, he can't be her true fiancé, since Alfred spoke with a possible suitor in the gallery. I hope Elara will clarify his relationship with Selene and the Addington family when we speak in the drawing room.

Six . . . Five . . .

Selene wouldn't have persisted in her flirtations with me if her hand was already spoken for, and the talk around town of an impending marriage would have met my ears soon enough, especially from Harold. He would have told me if Selene was to be married.

Four . . . Three . . .

Then again, secret engagements are common among the upper-privileged. I once knew a gentleman who was engaged for two years, and not even his mother knew of it. He courted two other women in secret as he built up his finances in order to marry the woman he sincerely loved.

Two . . .

I bow to a passing guest who flashes me a kind smile. I'm standing alone, wide-eyed and awkward.

Selene's posture hasn't changed, and I'm not sure she could become any more irate and stiff. She stands as still as a statue, listening attentively to Mr. Rothbottom.

Selene can't be engaged to this man.

Elara is toying with me. She must be.

One . . .

Carefully, I pass Selene, but she pays me no attention. I hear Mr. Rothbottom mentioning something about foolishness for mistreatment, and I break from the ballroom shortly after.

I hurry my steps, a growing excitement pushing me along. What could Elara have to say? Has Selene been in a secret engagement all along?

I enter the drawing room and close the door. Pale moonlight illuminates the dark room, brightening the closer I get toward an exposed window. I don't see Elara at first, and I'm startled when she steps into the moonlight from the shadows, pulling away a curtain.

"Tell me about Mr. Rothbottom," I say, keeping my distance.

Elara clasps her hands together and keeps her chin down. "I am a woman of propriety and respect my reputation greatly. And though tonight I have proven myself a bit out of character by drinking too much and now visiting secretly with you unescorted, when it comes to my family, I'm fine ignoring a few rules of propriety."

She wrings her hands and lets out a long sigh. "I'm sorry for any confusion I caused. I should have mentioned how Jerome Rothbottom is Selene's *old* fiancé. But an explanation is still required, should you question why Selene rejected your affections this morning."

"She told you about what occurred between us today?" My voice raises a little in pitch.

"Yes, which I hope you can forgive. We Addingtons have

our reasons for being guarded, and Selene and I have learned to rely upon one another."

Perhaps this is why Elara rejected Harold. Whatever these *reasons* are, they affect both women traumatically.

Sighing, I ask, "When was Selene engaged?"

"Five years ago." Her already somber demeanor turns grim. "Jerome Rothbottom is a distant cousin who has always had his eye on Selene, and my family was all too eager to accept a suitor whose bloodline was already known to be acceptable."

I sigh. It isn't uncommon to marry cousins. Half of Anna's Cove is probably intertwined tighter than a fancy tapestry.

Elara continues, "Shortly after her introduction to society at age sixteen, Jerome pursued her. Every girl was smitten with Jerome, but Selene was the center of his affections. They courted briefly and were engaged months before her seventeenth birthday. She acted as if it was some honor to be the future Mrs. Rothbottom. Many were envious, but Selene didn't mind."

I shift my weight, placing my hands upon my waist. "Why didn't she marry him? What changed?"

Gazing out the window, Elara leans against the sill and sighs. "The man of my sister's dreams turned out to be a nightmare. It started subtly with snide remarks and comments about her clothes or the way she spoke. Then he began expressing his strict expectations for Selene's behavior, speaking down to her as if she were a child for him to order about. Jerome grew jealous of her painting and other pursuits and demanded she give all her attention to him. That's when he started inviting her away for long weekends, insisting an escort was unnecessary as they were practically husband and wife already."

Elara hugs herself as if a cold wind rushed through her. Our eyes meet, and she shakes her head with shame. "She kept quiet because he convinced her it was improper to speak such disrespect toward a fiancé. Besides, he had a brilliant reputation on his side, and should Selene accuse him of not being as charming as everyone believed, the consequences would fall upon her, especially when it came to participating in any questionable behaviors. If they were to go away together, Jerome would be ignored, even lauded. Selene would be ruined."

"But he should have been responsible for his own actions."

Elara nods, relaxing a little. "Our society doesn't look upon a whorish woman with fondness or forgiveness. Meanwhile a man can display the worst kinds of irreverent behaviors and find redemption the moment he associates himself with someone far more virtuous. Believe me, Mr. Foster, there is a grave mistreatment from a society which worships the importance of a woman's subservience to the rules men write."

She fiddles with the hem of her sleeve, her attention upon the floor. "There was no relief for Selene. He could control her with just the threat of breathing a rumor. I saw the light within her fade. She was contentious and defended Jerome, fearing what he might do if he heard she'd said anything unflattering. In spite of it all, I can assure you she successfully sidestepped his improper advances and is still pure in spirit and body."

I sigh, stepping further into the light. "Even if she were quite the opposite, it wouldn't matter to me. I see the woman she is, and that is all I care about."

This lifts Elara's troubled spirit. "Selene was finally free of Jerome the moment my grandfather died. He was the one upholding the engagement contract, which became null and void the moment he took his last breath. Thankfully, my father banished Jerome from Addington Manor."

Until he showed up, possibly hoping for a second chance. Could Jerome be the suitor Alfred spoke to in the gallery?

"Could there be a chance your father would reconcile with Jerome if he made a more profitable offer?" I ask, my chest tightening at the thought.

Elara chuckles to herself. "I doubt it. Though my father has changed greatly since then, becoming more sentimental and merciful toward the less fortunate," she says, motioning to me, reminding me we're not friends. "If Jerome does intend to pursue

Selene once again, he better have a good reason to convince my father. I don't think any amount of money in the world will allow Jerome Rothbottom back into my father's good graces."

I scratch the back of my head, trying to make sense of Jerome's arrival.

"I appreciate you telling me all this, but I'm confused. Today you made it clear Addingtons don't marry for love, and yet you went out of your way to protect Selene and me against your mother's inquisition about being unescorted. Where do you stand regarding my pursuit of your sister?"

Elara straightens the front of her dress, her head still bowed. "It's true I do not like you, but not for reasons you may think. I helped you and Selene this morning because I believe at least one of us Addington women deserve a chance to be happily in love, even if socially it's unattainable. If you truly want Selene's hand, you must accept it in secret."

I contemplate Elara's suggestion. Though I don't like the idea of courting Selene in secret, it may be my only choice.

"You now know the shameful part of Selene's past," Elara says, "What you do with such information will reveal your devotion to her."

Elara's words bring a bittersweetness to my heart. She reminds me so much of Harold and the torment he puts himself through. I pity the woman. Her devotion to social expectations keeps her from loving Harold. Elara isn't happy in her engagement, and I refuse to have Selene suffer the same fate.

Composing herself, Elara steps toward the door. "I'm an engaged woman and shouldn't be associating with bachelors unescorted, thus I request you delay your exit while I return to the ballroom. I'm sure my mother is wondering where I am. She keeps a good eye upon me whenever Keagan is off on his own doing who knows what. I will bid you a good evening and ask you to pay no attention to me for the rest of the night."

"Agreed. Thank you, Elara," I say before she slips away.

CHAPTER 13

I enter the ballroom and search for Selene yet again, hoping her conversation with Jerome has ended. I need to speak with her. I need to know what Jerome's intentions are. Selene isn't with Elara, who now stands with Sophia and Diane, nor is she with her mother or any gathering of women. She's not dancing. She's gone.

My mind races over the various places she could have vanished to. I go to a footman at the base of the grand staircase, inquiring if Selene has gone upstairs. It would be easy to slip away and hide in her bedroom or any dark room for that matter.

The young man shakes his head politely. "I'm sorry. Miss Selene hasn't come this way all night."

I suspect she's fled to the hedge maze or rose garden. She often goes to these places when she needs a little time alone. Both are made of tall walls of foliage and flowers, which are in full bloom this time of year. It would take hours searching for her.

I glance at a nearby clock and see it's a little after nine. I must be quick, for the celebration will end within the hour, and Harold will wonder where I've gone.

Making my way toward the far end of the manor, I politely bow to Mr. Brent, who leaves the kitchen and watches me pass. Before he can ask where I am going, a servant hands him a large tray of pastries, distracting him as I slip out the back door and into the cool night air.

I welcome the change of scenery. The light of the moon's reach is blocked by the roof, encasing the back patio in a faded shadow. This social area consists of a large slab of cement topped with pots filled with ferns and sculpted shrubbery along with small stone benches for sitting. It's large enough to host a variety of intimate gatherings. Beyond the cold square are tall bushy shrubs which provide shade on sunny days.

I first scan the yard, but Selene is nowhere to be seen. The thought of searching the hedge maze is daunting, and I almost consider giving up.

"Oh, my head," a somber voice speaks from behind a tall shrub. "Too much wine. It always goes to my head."

Staggering away from behind a shrub is Elara's fiancé, Mr. Keagan Bottrell. He's a portly man with dirty blond hair and bright green eyes. The last time I met him was after the family returned from Elara's engagement party on the mainland. Mr. Bottrell hosted the celebration with plenty of wine and food to feed his guests for weeks.

Prior to that celebration he would occasionally grace Addington Manor with his presence in order to accompany Elara to social events required of her. Upon such visits Mr. Bottrell paid more attention to Selene, striking up conversations with her about the weather and other insignificant things.

"Mr. Bottrell, have you by chance seen Miss Selene?" I ask, walking to the man as he doubles over and dry heaves.

He motions for me to step back, his face turning four shades of red. He loosens his cravat and unbuttons his vest, allowing more air to enter his lungs. Finally standing, he fans himself, still teeming with embarrassment.

"Mr. Foster . . . what a lovely evening it is," he says, his face now a pale shade of green. "Fortunately, nobody has come this way. You are the first to grace this patio upon this lovely moonlit night."

He dabs his sweaty forehead and neck, clearing his throat before letting out a boisterous belch.

"Dearly pardon me," he says, leaning against the brick.

I glance at the rose garden, suspecting Selene could be there. The embarrassment she must feel, seeing Mr. Rothbottom after all these years.

"Mr. Bottrell, you look as though you need a walk."

The drunken man brushes the suggestion aside. "You have found me at my lowest of lows. Suspend the formalities and call me Keagan."

Keagan proceeds to tear at his collar. "It is so humid here, wouldn't you say?"

I don't want to leave the man alone, not in this state. I suspect he's been here quite a while.

"I should get Elara. She's been worried about you."

He laughs, his big belly bouncing. "You're such a tattle-prat. Elara couldn't care less if I were somewhere dead in the surrounding woods. She's probably relieved by my absence this evening."

Again I glance at the rose garden. "I cannot in my right mind leave you in such a state. I insist we venture on a small walk and get some fresh air. The rose garden has a suitable bench by the fountain. You can sit there comfortably and collect your bearings."

Mr. Bottrell brushes his matted hair from his face. "I'm aware of the layout of the rose garden, and though under different circumstances I'd find your offer highly unnecessary, I suppose you're right. I'm at my lowest, and you, kind sir, have extended a hand of service. It would be rude of me to reject your offer."

I carefully pull him away from the wall and steady him with my arms. He smells of brandy and body order mixed with the foulest cologne I've ever inhaled.

"Come now, dear man, to the rose garden," I say, clapping him on the back.

We begin our walk as a refreshing breeze gusts through the trees, making the tall limbs sway in the moon's light. In the distance, closer to the front of the manor, a band of servants are making preparations for fireworks. This makes my heart race a little more, for when the fireworks are lit, it will indicate the ending of the celebration.

Keagan finds his balance and keeps in step with me as I speedily distance myself from Addington Manor. Soon the cheerful music fades beneath the whisper of the wind.

I watch the clear sky. The faded light of twinkling stars brings little comfort to me.

Keagan finishes unbuttoning his shirt and fans himself with the stiff fabric. "I'll admit the grounds are lovely here. The rose garden is impressive. Elara and I took a walk there once."

We enter the rows of blooming flowers, Keagan taking in a deep breath before coughing.

"Sorry. The overwhelming smell of roses challenges my air passages. On a good day I can venture through the natural corridors with ease," he says, taking another deep breath through his mouth.

Ignoring him, I turn the corner and search for my dearest Selene.

From a bird's-eye view, the rose garden is constructed into a large circle. Like the hedge maze, it has dead-ends, various turns, and misleading openings, all leading toward a large water fountain at the center. The rose bushes tower over us, shrouding us in shadow as we move closer to the center.

"Why aren't you inside with Elara?" I ask, keeping him engaged.

Keagan slows his steps and catches his breath. "I care

little for such individual celebrations. Mina Island isn't like the mainland. It's too quiet here, and though I reside in Jared's Heath, I do prefer my summer cottages on the mainland."

The mention of multiple cottages reminds me how wealthy Keagan actually is. His family wealth stems from the textile business, which he inherited a year ago. I wouldn't be surprised if he provides the dark fabrics for Elara's many dresses.

Turning a few more corners, we reach the center of the garden, finding the peaceful scenery empty.

"Where is she?" I ask out loud, ignoring the portly man who conceals a cough.

Keagan rests his girth upon the stone bench and sighs. "Something tells me your charitable offer is serving two causes."

Frustrated, I sigh, and nod, relaxing my shoulders. "I need to find Miss Selene and speak with her. She was frightfully upset, and I want to make sure she's all right. She left the ballroom in a deplorable state after Mr. Rothbottom arrived."

"Dear man, don't you know you shouldn't worry? Women need their space. If she is upset, let her reach a level of calmness before returning. Women tend to be ruled by hysteria and need time for it to settle in their bodies."

He goes into a fit of coughing, stands once again, and takes a deep breath. "My apologies. May I suggest we extend this walk elsewhere?"

In agreeance with his suggestion of giving Selene a little time to calm herself, I nod and escort the man out of the garden at once.

Laughter from the servants and gathering guests echoes from the front of the manor. I'm tempted to search the group, but Keagan calls me away.

We continue walking, passing a few topiary lambs and a massive dog bounding after them. Walking a few more yards, beyond more sculpted shrubs, I become unfamiliar with my surroundings. I've never traveled this far from the manor and assume we will eventually reach the stone wall bordering the grounds.

"Is there something amiss between you and Elara that you wish to flee so far from the celebration?"

"You are quite observant, and I am drunk enough to be honest." Keagan chuckles. "Elara despises dancing. Elara can't stand my presence, and I can say I, too, despise hers."

My eyebrows raise at his confession. "But you're engaged to be married in a couple months."

Keagan stops to look me in the eye. "Good man, are you implying we should be marrying for love?" He lets out a boisterous laugh. "You hopeless romantics, no wonder you fill the poorhouses and die on the streets."

He continues to laugh, hardly containing himself. "Elara is a beautiful trinket to flash around whenever I need to flout my wealth and power. Other than that, I've no need of her. I've already granted her my blessing in taking on a lover with no questions asked."

I'm appalled but not surprised. This is what it means to be privileged. So many people matched into the unhappy marriages for the purpose of gaining wealth and influence.

"Is that all she is to you? A trinket? Do you not wish to have a companion in your wife?"

Keagan sees my detestation and stops laughing. "No, I do not. Trinkets are what all women are. They toil and chatter among themselves, socializing like hens in a coop. They are the ones who need to appear impressive, act demure, and keep a good face. Sure, we men have our responsibilities as well, but at the end of the day, we indulge and live off their dowries, enjoying the spoils of a legal arrangement.

"I've agreed to provide two years of expenses, and then I am free to do as I please with her monthly allowance."

My heart grows heavier as the truth of his words sink in. Privileged men see a woman as a trinket to be bought and displayed. If Jerome is capable of reconciling with Arthur, and presents a high enough offer, then I have no chance.

We pass another shrub, this one shaped into the form of a ghastly beast, perhaps a bear with its arms raised high.

"So you would say your engagement to Elara is more business oriented than emotional?" I ask, knowing the answer already.

He nods, almost slipping on the grass. "Yes, it was Mrs. Addington who suggested I court Elara. Most mothers make the social calls—"

"And what of Mr. Addington? Did he select you personally?" I stop and stare him directly in the eye. "Did he choose you for your wealth, knowing how it will bolster Elara's name among the social circles? Did he select you because the thought of wealth begetting wealth brings a charming smile to everyone's lips within this town?"

The drunken man shakes his head. "He actually didn't approve of the union whatsoever. He never stated a reason, but he wasn't invested in the situation to begin with."

I'm slowly putting together the pieces. If Arthur didn't approve, then why is Elara still engaged to marry Keagan? Is Mrs. Addington making the decisions? I compose myself and carry on with our walk as far away from the manor as possible.

"Were there no other suitors for Elara?" I press the question, making my feet walk faster, matching my thumping heart.

The man thinks for a moment, stroking his bare chin. "Yes. Mr. Taylor spoke with her father briefly about it. He's a man of significant enough means and status, and I was certain she liked him, so I was surprised when Elara recognized her duty, cut off all contact with Mr. Taylor, and accepted my proposal."

No wonder Elara turns to ice whenever I mention Keagan.

We come to a narrow path leading through a thick grove of willow trees. The breeze moves the curtain of branches all around us. The thin bristled leaves flutter and quake.

"I'm sorry to upset you, but I suspect Selene will follow in her sister's footsteps when it comes to the charming Mr. Rothbottom," Keagan says, pushing aside branches as he tries to keep up with me. "I believe I recognized him before I excused myself for the evening."

We stop in a clearing, the breeze now refreshing against my clammy skin.

"What do you know of them? Has Elara shared anything?"

He studies my face. "She's said nothing, but she doesn't have to. I've noticed the long glances between you and Miss Selene, but the wealthy enforce the Engagement Rule to discourage lower-class men from stealing away the upper-privileged women. I'm sure you have more than Mr. Rothbottom to oppose you. If you're lucky, she'll marry a wealthy gentleman who will allow her a lover. One can't fight against society, especially here in Anna's Cove."

I observe the full moon, recalling the extreme measures Henry has taken to keep himself in good standing with society. I might accept that economically my union to Selene would be frowned upon, but the thought of societal pressure forcing her to marry Jerome fills me with a deep pain. If she marries another, the only consolation I could hope for is her happiness, but she would be miserable with him.

"Where are we?" Keagan asks, interrupting my self-loathing.

I turn my gaze to the surrounding trees and the path we stand upon. I shrug and decide to continue following the path, curious of where it leads. Keagan reluctantly follows, letting out a tired sigh. We push through a few more walls of willow until we come to an open space unlike anything I've ever seen.

Tall stone pillars align evenly in a large circle, moss clinging to their weathered sides and filling in large cracks. I step from the path and onto freshly cut grass, the clippings brushed to the base of each stone. I carefully walk to the nearest column, observing flecks of silver reflecting the moon's light. There are seven pillars total, each varying in height but still towering over Keagan and me. Some are eroded to slanted points, while others are cracked and falling apart. Surrounding the circle of stones is a dense forest. Rays of moonlight break up the darkness, accentuating silhouettes of tree trunks and craggily branches. A misty fog blankets the fauna as crickets chirp in the distance.

"What is this place?" Keagan asks, his voice a low whisper.

I shrug. Selene has never allowed our long walks to go beyond the topiary. "I don't know. Perhaps ruins of an ancient castle."

I find a stone altar placed between two of the pillars to our right. It's made of a darker stone and stands about the height of a table. Behind the altar, moss covered steps glisten in the moon's light. Another set of steps are further north, blanketed in shadow by surrounding oak trees.

I inspect the altar, my mind racing now. Could this have been the place Henry killed the witch? Is his hidden cellar nearby?

My questions are interrupted by a low growl coming from the forest.

"What was that?" Keagan asks, searching the surrounding shadows. "I don't recall the Addingtons having any hounds."

The growl comes again, calling my attention to the trees behind one of the pillars. Carefully I step to Keagan's side, seeing the terrified look on his face.

Within the shadows something crouches close to the ground. At first I think it's a small animal startled by our presence and warning us to keep our distance. But then the creature stands upon two thick legs, rising to practically the height of a doorway.

I catch my breath, and my knees lock.

The beast's long arms reach to its knees, and its body rises and falls with each exhale. It remains still, hidden in the shadows, but is clearly making its presence known.

"Should we run?" Keagan asks, his voice still quiet but shrill.

I keep a close observation on the creature, wondering what it is. My pulse quickens and the hairs on the back of my neck prickle. Its eyes remind me of a man's, circular and encompassing. But the most disturbing thing about them, the most unnatural characteristic, is the glowing red color against the void of shadow.

A snarl escapes the figure, more aggressive now, causing Keagan and I to quake.

"Devin," Keagan says nervously, "what is that thing?"

I swallow hard, remembering where I've seen those eyes, sinewy limbs, and pointed black ears. I gawk at the sharp teeth and long snout. I'd locked the image away in the back of my mind, shrouded in myth and whispers.

"It's not a thing, exactly, but who," I reply.

Keagan shoots me an acidic look. "What are you talking about?"

I take one last deep breath, steadying my racing heart. "It's Henry Addington."

CHAPTER 14

I stare at the monster, my legs as heavy as lead. I've faced danger before, life threatening even, but I've never seen such a creature, and I'm not sure how to react.

"Henry Addington?" Keagan repeats. Squinting his eyes, he takes a lingering look. "You mean the deranged man who murdered his sons two-hundred years ago?" Keagan returns his gaze to the red-eyed shadow and instinctively steps back. "You're mad."

Still within the shadows, the beast growls again, prompting me to slowly back away. "It's Henry Addington, cursed to punish those who aren't worthy of the Addingtons' social circle. The old woman was right. Man beasts are real."

BOOM!

The sky fills with flickering red and white light.

The fireworks scream into the dark sky, competing with the moon's light and announcing their end with a thunderous boom.

I return my gaze to the forest, finding the monster gone.

More fireworks burst, blanketing the trees in red light.

Keagan's chest heaves. "I don't like this one bit. Perhaps we should run," he says, his voice shaky and shrill.

Without any thought, he dashes toward the path leading away from the circle of stone pillars.

"Keagan, wait!" I call.

I dare not linger nor look behind me as I race through the wall of willows and follow Keagan toward Addington Manor. My legs pump harder as my mind races. Why didn't the creature attack? He could have torn us to shreds, and yet he remained within the shadows, growling, warning us.

I don't know if I believe it was Henry Addington, or at least his beastly form. But it must be him. I can't think of any other creature looking so hideously frightening.

I break from the willow trees, passing the topiary into familiar territory. People are returning inside to gather their things and leave.

Keagan is doubled over on the grass, vomiting and catching his breath. I take hold of his arm, urging him into a sprint toward the back patio.

The nearest door of the manor is within my sight, my legs pumping harder and harder.

"We're almost there," I say.

We reach the patio, step over the stone bench, and break through the back door.

Keagan trips over me as we both crash to the floor, startling Mr. Brent and a couple kitchen servants.

"There's a monster out there!" I yell much louder than I expected.

My voice draws the attention of a few guests, but Mr. Brent shields me from their view.

"My goodness, have you no decency?" he scolds.

Snapping his fingers, two footmen pick Keagan up while another helps me to my feet.

I point to the door. "I saw Henry. I saw him . . . I saw . . . the stone pillars . . . Henry was there.”

The immediate mention of Henry causes Mr. Brent’s eyes to widen. “I think you two have had too much to drink,” he says, his lips pursed into their usual frown. “Mr. Foster, you know you shouldn’t be going beyond the rose garden.”

“I was helping Mr. Bottrell calm his spirits,” I say between gasps.

The butler looks at Keagan and motions to the man as he rests upon the nearest chair. “Calm his spirits indeed. Look at him. He’s as drunk as a wench on All Confession’s Day.”

I can’t disagree with him. Keagan is pale and mumbling to himself.

“It was a man beast,” I say, waving my hands about. “The one in Selene’s painting.”

Mr. Brent’s stern glare narrows, and he steps between me and Keagan. His gray eyes burn into mine as his cheeks flush with embarrassment. “You’re drunk and seeing things.”

I’m offended by his assumption of my state of mind. “Mr. Brent, I have barely touched a drop, and I know about the story you told Ms. Taylor years ago.”

The man harumphs, patting my arm before telling a footman to get Keagan a cup of black coffee. He ushers me away from the kitchen and walks me to the ballroom.

“I told the story to Ms. Taylor in order for her to find me mysterious and intriguing. I was young and foolish, and I wanted the attention of a wealthy woman. Henry Addington has been dead for centuries. He was a tyrant, and I will say nothing else of him. How do you know it wasn’t some servants fooling around in the forest?”

Carefully studying his face, I stop him. “Jamison, I know what I saw. As clear as day, I know what I saw.”

“Enough.” Mr. Brent leans closer as if to conceal a secret. I anticipate a confirmation of what I saw, but the butler sighs and says, “You both missed the Grand Toast, and guests are already departing for the evening. Mr. Taylor asked for you a few minutes ago."

"I know what I saw. And though I'm shaken to my core, I want you to know it doesn't frighten me away from Selene."

"Are you listening to yourself? Strong drink will make a man see whatever he wants to see, do you understand? If you're not drunk, then something else has occupied your thoughts. That would not bode well for your future prospects."

We stand in silence. Why doesn't he believe me? I've only confirmed his story to be true, why can't he reassure me I'm not crazy?

"There is your friend. Good evening, Mr. Foster," Mr. Brent says, excusing himself and returning to Keagan, leaving me at the threshold to the ballroom.

I glimpse Harold in the ballroom, and our eyes meet, but my attention is distracted when the gallery door opens and Arthur steps out, followed by Alfred and Jerome. They must have already met and discussed Selene's engagement.

I study Arthur's face, hoping for an idea of how the meeting went, but he avoids eye contact with everyone around him and moves quickly into the parlor.

Harold marches directly to me. "Where have you been? Miss Blueshire overheard that Jerome Rothbottom has come to claim Selene's hand. I didn't believe it until I saw him and then I tried to find you to see if you'd heard."

I nod and start making my way to the front door.

Harold's face softens. "I'm so sorry." The heavy aroma of alcohol on his breath washes over me. Even Harold understands my impossible obstacle.

"Your aunt was right about Henry. He does exist, and he's a terrible monster," I say passively.

Harold laughs. "We've got to get you home and to bed. You've had too much to drink and too much to care about throughout this day. Your mind is spent."

Glaring, I shake my head. "There's a monster out there right now, waiting to prey upon people. The Culling is real."

Surprised by my persistence, Harold lifts his hands in surrender. "All right, all right. The man beast is real. Now can we go?"

I slump my shoulders in defeat. Nobody will believe me. How could they? To them, man beasts are monsters in stories. But I saw one. Henry Addington exists.

Reluctantly, I follow Harold to the edge of the grand lobby and wait for the Blueshires to join us. Mr. Blueshire is bidding his farewell to Marcus as Penny leaves the ballroom with her friends.

After concealing a yawn, I rub my eyes. Maybe the alcohol has affected my brain, molding all the events into one muffled fever dream.

"Mr. Foster," Mrs. Addington shouts from across the lobby.

She motions for me to join her, and I hesitate to do so until Harold nudges me to obey.

"Mrs. Addington," I say, perking up my face as to not draw attention to my addled thoughts. "I'm about to leave with Mr. Taylor. Is there something you need?"

The woman cups her hands together over her chest and sighs. "I want you to join us for one final toast, just the family and some close friends. I know how fond my husband has become of you, and I wish to surprise him by inviting you."

I glance at Harold, but Eliza touches my arm, giving me a pleasant smile.

"Please. It will be a great honor to my husband if you'd join us. It's something quite intimate and a dear tradition. I noticed you weren't in attendance with the Grand Toast. I'd feared you'd already left."

"No, not quite." I take one last glance at Harold as the Blueshires stand beside him and wait.

Eliza tightens her grip upon my arm. "I want you to attend as a way of apologizing to both of you. I can be quite stern and set in my ways, but I must try to understand my husband's reason in taking you as an apprentice. He was so heartbroken after Quintin left; I couldn't help but wonder if you were the replacement of our son.

"I know it sounds harsh, but that made me angry with Arthur and, to an extent, you. But now, with Quintin's return and seeing how happy Marcus is with his beloved Diane, I can't help but open my heart to accepting you as a dear friend of the family. I'm so grateful you came tonight. Please, please allow me to accommodate your ride home after our final, traditional toast has come to an end."

To reject Mrs. Addington at this point of vulnerability would be cruel.

I take one last glance at Harold and motion for them to go on without me. This prompts a smile on Harold's face as he pushes the Blueshires toward the front door.

"Excellent," Eliza says, clapping her hands. "We'll have the family toast in the gallery once all the guests have left. Until then, enjoy a few more pastries and wine. You look quite pale."

She shuffles off to bid a few guests goodbye, leaving me standing alone.

Yes, I think a glass of wine will be helpful in calming my shaking body. It could help me indeed.

CHAPTER 15

The ballroom isn't as stuffy now with fewer guests stomping about. The musicians have already put their instruments away, helping themselves to any remaining pastries and glasses of warm wine. A handful of servants carefully clear the tables, some lifting empty glasses into buckets, others removing the lacey tablecloths for cleaning in the morning. Two servants lower the first chandelier and start snuffing out the candles and blowing away the smoke.

I take a glass of wine and walk to the nearest window.

The moon shines like a lantern over the land, bathing everything in a dull blue light. I gaze at my reflection before casting my sight upon the swaying trees.

"What a beautiful celebration this has been. Time truly does fly when one is enjoying the moment among friends," a strangely familiar voice speaks from behind me. I try to remember where I've heard the voice, and then it comes to me.

The gallery. The potential suitor.

I turn, lifting my chin to look upon the infamous Jerome Rothbottom.

Jerome has a similar build to Henry's monstrous form, with broad shoulders and a lengthy height. His long black hair now falls freely behind his thick neck, a few inches past his collar. With a square jaw and triangular nose, he's undeniably handsome. A few servants stare at him a little longer than they should. Their cheeks flush with heat when he peers in their direction.

Jerome bows and extends his hand. "I'm Jerome Rothbottom, a friend of the Addingtons. And you are?"

I'm pretty sure he knows who I am. I wouldn't be surprised if my name was mentioned casually by Alfred when presenting Jerome to Arthur as Selene's wealthy suitor.

I ignore his hand and sip the rest of my wine instead.

"Devin Foster, Arthur Addington's apprentice."

This title must entertain him, for a half smile washes over Jerome's face, his white teeth reflecting the moon's light beaming through the window. "Eliza pointed you out as a regular presence in the manor, so I thought it would be wise to say hello. I expect we'll see each other frequently in the months to come."

I hide my disbelief, controlling every muscle in my face. Arthur has agreed for Selene to marry him.

"Frequently?" I repeat, keeping my voice devoid of any emotion.

His nose crinkles, and his half smile deepens. "Arthur is taking into consideration my offer to marry Selene. Do you know her well?"

His radiant blue eyes grow cold as he lifts a single eyebrow.

This horrible man . . . no . . . this boy, this insignificant dot has done damage to my dearest Selene. His words have bruised her precious heart, once broken the vivacious spirit she possesses. Whether it's the wine, or the sheer exhaustion, something primitive boils within me, wanting to reprimand him for his abuse.

"I would say Miss Selene and I are quite fond of one

another," I reply as calmly and gentlemanly as possible. "We have shared long conversations about society and all it entails. She's extraordinary and important to me, and I would hate for anything unworthy of her kindness to befall her. May I ask how you have come to Selene's acquaintance?"

He doesn't answer right away, but motions for us to sit at the nearest table instead. But I don't want to sit. I want to go home. I want to pretend this day never happened. I want to undo everything I've said and done. I want to forget all about it.

My grip tightens around my glass until my hand starts to shake. Jerome notices and clears his throat.

"Are you all right, sir?" A servant says, respectfully offering to take my glass. I force a smile while handing over the chalice.

"Thank you, Nina," I say, feeling a sense of accomplishment for knowing the servant's name. It's a redeeming quality to treat the help with respect, seeing them as people and nothing less. I assume such a quality is lost on the pompous Jerome, as he probably sees everyone as something to manipulate.

"Nina," Jerome says the name as if he's heard it for the first time. "How is Kingsley enjoying his new position in Hallsent?"

Nina curtsies, her sweet voice rising with delight. "He very much enjoys tending to Mr. Ledger. Have you heard of him?"

Jerome shakes his head. "Unfortunately not. I haven't been to Hallsent in months. But when I'm in town again, I'll be sure to send my greetings."

Nina giggles. "Why, thank you, Mr. Rothbottom. Such a thoughtful gentleman, you are." She shuffles off with a skip in her step.

Jerome watches Nina leave the ballroom, leering at the swing in her hips.

"She was always a kind woman," he says, returning his gaze upon me. "I do believe we should sit and speak for a moment, if you please." He squints from a forced grin.

"Why the persistence?"

I don't move.

My disobedience is creating quite the tension, but Jerome doesn't give up. "I only wish to know the man Arthur thinks so highly of. When he spoke of you earlier this evening, I could see the pride in his eyes. You've made quite an impression on him. I've never had the luxury of receiving a second look from Arthur, and here you've attained a soft spot in his heart."

The only thought racing through my mind is how Arthur could agree to Selene's engagement to Jerome, who, according to Elara, disregarded the rules of propriety to a harmful degree. Though Selene and I would venture on our own, I would never jeopardize her reputation or attempt to interfere with her virtue.

Jerome walks closer to the bare table, a few chairs tucked beneath it. He pulls out a chair and takes a seat. "Sit, please."

I'm fully aware of the social rules when in the presence of someone greater in status than I. It was one of the first things Arthur taught me before beginning my lessons in accounting. I should sit to show my respect. If only I had respect for the man.

But I should also be a better man and not stoop to the level of a ruffian.

Reluctantly, I join him. The moon's light is brighter now as the second chandelier is lowered, its candles stifled.

I sit in silence, keeping my eyes downcast. Jerome's presence infuriates me. The thought of his abuse forces me to hate him.

Politely, he sighs and deepens his tone. "I feel the need to clarify my association with the Addingtons. I was once engaged to Selene, but complications arose. There were things I did and said that weren't becoming of a man of my station, and the arrangement was called off."

"There is no need for clarification."

"But there is," his voice raises, and he clenches his hands. "I saw Elara leave the ballroom and you following shortly after. I make no claim of suspicion between the two of you. Elara is bound by social duty to uphold her engagement, and Mrs. Addington has told me how fond you are of Selene."

My knee bounces rapidly when he mentions Mrs. Addington's knowledge of my affections. I've concluded I'm terrible at hiding my emotions.

Jerome continues, "I believe I was the reason for your secret meeting with Elara. My past is all but tainted by my actions, and I can imagine what Elara has told you. I want to assure you I'm a changed man and will never endanger Selene. She's all I can ever think about, and with her absence I've realized what a fool I was in mistreating her. If I'm able to marry her, she'll be well taken care of."

If? So an engagement contract hasn't been finalized. I grip my leg to keep it from bouncing. The thought of him married to Selene makes me sick, but that *if* allows me to control my rampant thoughts of him bringing any harm to her and steady my breathing.

"Mr. Rothbottom, I am but a humble apprentice and you a highly privileged man. Though we share a common affection for Miss Selene, I don't believe Mr. Addington will allow you to take her hand in marriage. He's not a fool and severed your ties with the family for a good reason. I'm under the impression a sincerely changed man would never claim his penitent heart but display it through benevolent actions." The words fall from my lips without any thought to repercussions. If I'm to embarrass myself, at least I'm doing it for the honor of my beloved.

Jerome's jaw tenses. "I am a changed man. Losing Selene made me realize the darkness within me. I'm not the same person I once was. You understand how difficult it is bolstering one's name within a tightknit society. I arrived by invitation of Alfred Addington, and I'm still met with scathing looks as sharp as daggers. It's been five years. You're an apprentice, a man breaking free of his social stigma associated with the impoverished. We share a commonality as men attempting to shed our previous lives for a much improved one. You of all people can clearly sympathize."

Me of all people? Does he really think we have so much

in common? I'm reminded every day how insignificant I am because I have so little money and humble means of shelter, a condition I was born into. He faces the consequences of his own choices.

"I do understand the difficulty of shaking free of one's past," I say, keeping a steady voice, "but what you have done, regardless of your penitent heart, makes you an undeserving candidate for Selene's hand. You cannot fool me with your attempts for sympathy. You've not been unfairly victimized by social heresy but by your own selfish decisions. I would never intentionally bring pain or suffering to Selene. I would sacrifice my own comfort and happiness first."

The sympathetic look on his face fades. "So what Alfred says is true. You do wish to infringe upon the Addington legacy."

I lean forward, clenching my hands into tight fists beneath the table. "I want what's best for Selene."

He leans as well, baring his teeth as he speaks. "So do I, and I can actually provide it." He shakes his head with disgust. "You think she could sincerely love you? Selene doesn't know what true love is. She is a child in need of protection. She freely gives her heart away without thinking of the consequences." He sits in his chair, folding his arms across his chest. "Let me see if this sounds familiar. She showed you the secret loft connected to the recreation room?"

My tense shoulders involuntarily droop. How does he know about that?

Jerome chuckles with satisfaction, sensing my confusion. "Has Selene invited you on secret rendezvous, allowed you to steal kisses in the library, and guided you on long walks in the hedge maze?"

I slump in my chair, my eyes adjusting to the dim light surrounding us.

Jerome is thrilled at my reaction. "Do you think you are the only one? I was engaged to her. I know more about Selene than you can possibly imagine."

We stare at each other in silence. There's a significant tightening in my chest, and an angry lump forms at the base of my throat at his attempt to slander Selene as foolish and untrustworthy.

Of course I'm not the only one. I don't care how many suitors she's had or how many hearts she has broken with her soft gaze and gentle touch. Nor do I concern myself with how many men she's danced with or made impossible promises to. It's what being young and in love is all about.

I'm not a fool, nor am I blind.

And despite Jerome's wretched ploy to make me think less of my dearest Selene, I still declare my love for her with all energy of heart. I love her despite the obstacles which stand between us.

"It's time for the final toast," Mrs. Addington's voice echoes through the almost empty ballroom. "Come along to the gallery you two."

We both stand, each sizing each other up.

Jerome steps away from the table and bows respectfully with a smirk. "After you, Mr. Foster."

CHAPTER 16

Jerome and I enter the gallery, attracting the attention of everyone present. I slowly turn my gaze toward the secret cellar door, finding the thick rug placed over it. The room is now lit with several candles and oil lamps set on display tables scattered throughout the room. On the main wall, a grand portrait showcases Henry Addington sitting in an oversized wooden chair. Henry's dark human eyes stare directly at me. I shudder at the thought of the old man transforming into the cruel beast he is now. I can't forget what I saw in the woods and consider myself lucky that he didn't chase after us as prey.

All Addington members stand beside their partners. Both Arthur and Selene exchange glances with one another as Eliza cheerfully greets us.

"Jerome, welcome," Eliza says. She embraces him, pressing her cheek against his. "You may take your place beside Alfred."

In the distant corner a servant is stoking a fire. It burns with intense flames fed by coal and logs of cedar.

Mrs. Addington faces me. "Mr. Foster, if you could stand beside Selene, it would be much appreciated. I'm so grateful to have you here."

She escorts me to Selene's side. I try not to look smug about joining Selene while Jerome is paired with Alfred. Eliza respectfully bows to Arthur. She leans closer to me, whispering, "My surprise has been accomplished. Mr. Addington didn't know you'd be part of this, nor Selene. Oh, how I do like keeping everyone in suspense."

Selene clasps her hands in front of her, keeping quiet as I take my place by her side. Moments pass in silence as we exchange subtle nods. Selene glances at Jerome only to sigh and turn her gaze elsewhere. I rock on my heels, fighting the urge to speak to her. There's so much I want to ask, but I don't want to offend her.

Finally, Selene breaks the silence and leans closer to me. Her fingertips barely touch my shoulder, catching Jerome's attention from across the room.

"My apologies for abandoning you on the dance floor," she whispers. "Elara told me you two spoke with one another."

I nod, avoiding eye contact with her as I keep a close watch on Jerome and Alfred whispering to one another. "There is no need to apologize. I understand why you'd be upset with Jerome's arrival. I'm grateful for the chance I had to dance with you tonight."

A soft smile graces her lips before she clears her throat.

She leans closer to my side. "I, too, enjoyed our time together. It was a happy moment during a day that has gradually worsened, and I don't see it changing for the better."

I'm ashamed to think I've added to Selene's dreadful day. I refuse to dwell upon this morning, and my thoughts linger on our moment on the dance floor. I'm not sure what Selene would have told me had we had the chance to speak privately, but I believe it would have been pleasant.

"I'm sure the toast will be brief, and the night will soon

draw to an end," I politely say.

My words prompt Selene to look into my eyes. "This dreaded toast. You should have left with Harold," she whispers.

Naturally, my hand brushes against hers. "I do feel as though I'm imposing. I agreed to participate out of respect for your mother. She was rather insistent."

"She has a way of using social expectations as tools of manipulation, something I'm not fond of."

I gently touch her shoulder, carefully avoiding contact with her skin. "Perhaps after the toast we can continue our conversation that Mr. Rothbottom's appearance interrupted."

Her nose crinkles as she tilts her head. "I suppose that would be all right."

Eliza motions for everyone to quiet down, insisting the women stand on the right side of each gentleman.

Though everyone appears happy and a little tired, something doesn't feel right. One footman begins serving each guest a glass of white wine while another serves each Addington family member some red wine.

"Here you go, sir," one of the footmen says. I clasp the narrow neck between my fingers and swirl the fragrant contents. I detect a hint of sage and thyme. This isn't the same wine served at the celebration. Harold's wine is sweeter with a pinch of citrus.

I watch the footman holding the tray of red wine approach Jerome and Alfred. Both stand closest to the fire, the flames highlighting their chiseled features. Each are given a glass before the servant scurries out of the room. I'm curious why Jerome didn't receive the same white wine as the invited guests until I recall he is a distant cousin.

I watch each couple move into a designated place as Eliza moves about the room forming everyone into a large circle.

Keagan looks tired but put back together. He reluctantly stands beside Elara, keeping as much distance as he can between them. The man swirls his wine and inhales the lifting aroma. He looks around the room, admiring the various paintings hung on the walls. Elara pays little attention to Keagan as she politely smiles at everyone and stands in silence.

I turn my attention to Marcus and Diane. They stare at one another intensely, as if lost in a secret conversation. Marcus carefully removes one of the red roses from her hair, kissing the petals before tucking it into his pocket. Diane blushes and steps closer to her fiancé, their fingers intertwining at her side. Such a handsome couple they are.

Quintin stands beside his wife, kissing her cheek and holding her hand. He's quite affectionate toward her, lifting her spirits. At one point Quintin makes a silly face, eliciting a playful smirk from his wife. She tries to hide it from Eliza's wandering eye.

I recall Eliza mentioning earlier to Mrs. Kensy of Quintin's intentions to leave Sophia, but I see nothing amiss between them. Both stand with exaggerated posture, politely nodding to Eliza as she moves Quintin closer to Sophia. Once the old woman makes her way to Elara and Keagan, Sophia and Quintin relax and continue silently teasing one another, quietly giggling from time to time.

From the corner of my eye, I notice Arthur staring directly at me. He grinds his teeth and ignores his wife. Something is on his mind, and from the stern look on his face, it isn't good. He doesn't look away when I return his gaze.

"Is your father all right?" I ask Selene, "He appears unhappy to see me."

Looking at her father, Selene shakes her head. "He's tired. Late nights have begun to take their toll on him, but it's been a long evening for us all."

She straightens her back and looks at her mother, letting me know she has no intention of continuing our conversation. I wonder if Mr. Rothbottom's presence has anything to do with it.

As I glance over those present, I think of the strange details of this tradition. My mind wanders to Ms. Taylor's tale about the fateful night Anna was murdered. The horrible beast I saw gives some validity to the tale, though I still don't understand why it didn't attack Keagan and me.

If the tale is true, then tonight a Culling will take place. I suppress a smile at the thought of this being the Culling, though I know, according to Ms. Taylor's account, that I wouldn't be invited to such an event. I've not yet announced my intention to court Selene, and the tradition was for fiancés and potential suitors.

I indulge in the morbid story and wonder which of the unfortunate guests would be forced to participate. I doubt Sophia will be part of the Culling. She's already married to Quintin.

I smirk at Keagan, wondering if he'd be fast enough to escape the vile clutches of the horrid beast.

When gazing at Diane, I believe she would survive. Though I don't know much about her, she looks like a clever woman.

But as my thoughts linger upon Jerome, the blighter, I can't help but take pleasure in imaging his heart being ripped from his chest. I suppose, come the start of the new week, I'll hear how tragically he lost his life by the hand of a wild beast.

Such thoughts prompt a smirk on my face. I think the wine has finally mingled with my exhaustion and distorted my good morals. But I have nothing to worry about. I will not be participating in any deranged family tradition tonight.

I am a humble apprentice who is as insignificant as a dot on a page. They'd never trust me with so large of a secret. Honestly, I only wish to leave as soon as the toast is finished and be done with the Addingtons for now.

"We're ready," Eliza speaks. She takes her place at Arthur's side. She flashes a satisfied smile when looking over everyone in the room.

As she gives a lengthy report of the well-celebrated evening, I notice the gloom on Arthur's face as he still stares at me. I try to ignore his gaze as Mrs. Addington continues to speak.

"For centuries this traditional toast has upheld the knowledge of how we are stronger when united in a common belief. With the upcoming union of Marcus and Diane, it is our hope you always respect the values which have kept our family in excellent social standing and great wealth.

"The power which comes by these means provides a good life for the next generation. May your thoughts always press upon how our actions must maintain our values from generation to generation."

She lifts her glass. "Remember, when we speak of drinking to one's value, we sip," Eliza says with a cheerful smile. She turns to Arthur, motioning to him to step forward. "Our patriarch, will provide the toast."

This breaks Arthur's attention from me, and he steps into the circle and clears his throat. He looks over his family, steadily holding his glass but not raising it. His thoughts are distracted.

"Arthur," Eliza says, "the toast."

There's a long pause as he holds his glass up, prompting everyone to do the same. His gaze lingers over his children, stopping at Quintin. A look of guilt washes over the man, and he lowers his glass.

"I'm sorry. I can't do this," Arthur says, momentarily stepping out of the circle. "I'm too overcome with emotion to speak. My apologies for this embarrassment."

Eliza steps forward as we all lower our glasses and exchange confused glances. "Then I shall do it. Be it we are married, we're practically one in the same." She faces Alfred. "With your permission of course."

Alfred nods, motioning for her to continue.

She raises her glass, and we do the same. "There have been enough family toasts to remember the words." Eliza looks at everyone in the room and stands tall. She clears her throat and says, "For centuries, Addingtons have thrived upon making the wisest selections in partners who strengthen our ties to good wealth and handsome breeding. Marcus has made a wonderful selection with Diane. We look forward to their future marriage in the months to come. May they build their marriage upon trust, respect, and loyalty. Let us drink to the happy couple's union."

I lower my cup. My tongue tingles a little, as if something cold lingers upon its surface. The tingle continues down my throat, causing me to clear it. Keagan does the same, noting how sharp the after taste is.

Ignoring us, Eliza slowly leaves Arthur's side. Her eyes pan over all who stand around her. "With a marriage comes trust. It is a wife's duty to trust her husband will provide all the necessities of life and protect her from those who would do her harm. Trust is the foundation to all good marriages. May Marcus be a good husband and never break the trust of a good husband. Let us drink to Marcus."

After sipping his drink, Marcus kisses Diane's cheek and grins.

Keagan clears his throat once more, prompting Elara to roll her eyes and whisper something in his ear. In reaction, Keagan sighs and squares his shoulders.

Eliza continues. "Respect is the next quality which strengthens a married couple's union. There is much to be expected of both husband and wife, but it is the wife who will represent the heart of her family. If she is met with any disrespect from her husband, may she be wise to remind him, with a gentle touch and tender word, the significance of her existence. For a woman will always maintain greater respect for her husband, but it is he who should never forget who brings forth life and beauty in their marriage. Let us drink to Diane."

I lower my glass, noticing Sophia sharing a kind glance with Quintin. She momentarily cradles herself and straightens her dress. Elara also notices the interaction and a look of suspicion washes over her face.

"And now we draw to the end of this wonderful celebration," Eliza says, beaming from ear to ear. "For loyalty is ideal in all relations. Not only must Marcus and Diane remain loyal to one another, through good times and bad times, but they must also remain loyal to our great family name."

Selene slowly lowers her cup and looks at her father. She

remains quiet but shakes her head a little. Quintin also glances at his father, as if Eliza has spoken out of turn. Arthur ignores his children and keeps his eyes downcast.

I don't understand what Eliza has said to prompt such a reaction from the two. Elara appears elated, strangely overcome with a sense of pride as her mother proceeds to face Henry's portrait.

"For centuries the Addingtons have kept in favor of all who reside in Anna's Cove. It was Henry Addington who believed there was power in wealth and status. Those who have remained loyal to our family ideals have been blessed with abundance. May the Addington traditions carry on as reminders of how trust, respect, and loyalty unify us against those who would oppose our ideals. May we live up to the Addington name with pride and honor. Let us drink to the one who provided all we have today. Let us drink to Henry Addington."

Marcus slowly finishes his drink and glares at Henry's portrait. Diane shares the same sentiment as she lowers the glass from her lips.

Once Eliza finishes her drink, she lets out a happy cheer and walks her glass to the fireplace. She tosses it into the flames and smiles at Alfred and Jerome, who also give a cheer before doing the same. Keagan cheers as well but stops the moment Elara guides him toward the fire. One by one, everyone hurls their glasses into the fire.

Jerome remains by the fireplace, keeping quiet and distant from the family. He stares at Selene, but she pays little attention to him, occasionally glancing his way but often keeping her eyes downcast.

Eliza links arms with Diane and walks her through the gallery. She states how delighted she is to have Diane as a future daughter-by-law. The two women share their thoughts about the upcoming wedding. Sophia watches them and frowns when Eliza pays no attention to her.

Quintin comforts his wife, placing an arm around her as

they slowly walk out of the gallery.

A strange heaviness overcomes me as reality sets in. The day is finished, and I'm no better a man than I was when I woke this morning. Intending to exclaim my love for Selene, I've only been met with rejection and discouragement. In comparison to Jerome Rothbottom I have already lost Selene's hand, for money speaks louder than love. The only good thing about this day was Harold's words of encouragement, though I'm still not sure he's deserving so much credit. I still blame him for planting such fantastical thoughts in the first place.

I remain close to Selene. My heart races a little as our eyes meet. Her beautiful tan complexion glows in the firelight.

"Shall we take a walk?" I ask, guiding her out of the gallery.

She follows, silently walking beside me. We make our way toward the main lobby as two servants lower the grand chandelier to snuff its candles. Everyone else remains in the gallery conversing with one another. Selene and I are alone, making it easier for me to speak freely without judgement from Jerome or Eliza.

Selene stares at the red carpet. Like her father, she appears distracted by something.

"Before you express whatever it was you were going to tell me earlier tonight, I must express the thoughts lingering on my mind about Jerome."

"There is no need," Selene says.

"Something Jerome said has ignited an unwanted curiosity within me," I say, stammering a little.

"What is it?" she asks, her hands fidgeting with the hem of her sleeves.

I fan myself with my collar as sweat beads along the back of my neck. My heart beats rapidly, and I pause, leaning against a nearby table. I try to focus on her beautiful face.

"Did he jump when you took him to the roof?"

She looks at me, dumbfounded. Her whole face relaxes. "No, Jerome didn't jump either. Instead, he chided me, called me irresponsible, and demanded I never play such horrible games ever again."

Laughter echoes from the gallery, prompting Selene to take me by the arm and guide me farther down the hall. We enter the main lobby, her heels clicking on the marble floor. The servants have finished stifling each candle and carefully hoist the chandelier back into place. White whisps of smoke trail into the air.

Selene whispers while ignoring the servants. "Jerome was condescending. He reminded me to put away childish things and be a more dignified woman. He never liked my paintings or sketches, seeing them as wastes of time. He expected more from me." She shakes her head and fiddles with her choker. "At least you had a suitable reason not to jump, and I've already apologized."

We pause, hiding away from prying eyes and lingering in the dim light. I take her hands into mine. "I'm sorry for acting foolish. Once Elara told me about Jerome and the possibility of your father reconciling—"

Selene stops me with a kiss. Her hand finds the back of my neck as she closes her eyes and takes a deep breath. My hands rests at her waist as I pull her closer, my fingers tracing the small of her back. Her fingernails comb through my hair as her lips part.

Breathless, she pulls away, resting her cheek against mine. "You have always seen me as no one else has," she whispers in my ear. "I am truly grateful for you, Devin. I wish things were different for us. I wish we could continue living our beautiful dream."

She gives me no opportunity to respond but kisses me again. Tears wet her cheeks as she clings to me. My thoughts grow hazy, and I can't tell if it's the alcohol or Selene's kiss which overwhelms me. As she steps away, the room appears darker, and everything is out of focus.

"Selene," I whisper, balancing myself against the front door.

"I'm so sorry," she says, shielding her quivering chin with her hand.

I try to speak, but my whole body begins to tremble. What's happening to me? What was in the wine? My mouth dries, and I lose my strength. Falling to my knees, I try to stand, but my arms give way. I collapse to the cold marble floor. The room is spinning out of control. I call to Selene one last time before everything goes black.

CHAPTER 17

I was once told how when we die, we return to the darkness from which we were born and remain in such a dreadful state of mind until we're driven mad. But others have claimed, like birth, though we are surrounded by darkness, eventually there is a light, and it is this light which ignites the coil within our souls as we pass into the Great Hall of the Creator.

Whether I am dreaming or dead, I find myself lost in memory, whirling about as if caught in a treacherous squall. Colors behind my eyelids blend like smudges on a soiled paper. Sounds are muffled. I'm numb to all feeling against my skin, and I don't recognize anything by their smell. Time is irrelevant, but as the storm surrounding me worsens, I hear a familiar voice speaking words I had long forgotten.

My eyes open and observe my beloved mother lying on her death bed. Her sunken chest rises slowly with each deep inhale. Her transparent skin clings to her bones. The shape of her skull protrudes as she tries to keep her heavy eyes open.

My sensations return, filling me with dread and anxiety.

"Quiet now," my mother speaks, her voice a low rasp as it scratches through her tiny throat. Each word is agonizing for her to develop. She takes her time to breathe, her words staggering from her mouth as her head rests on a flat pillow. "You were always a better man than your father."

I set my hand upon her fingers, holding them as if I were holding a bundle of sticks. "You mustn't speak, Mother. You must rest."

We sit in the small room above the local chapel. The pastor has been kind enough to let my mother die in peace and safety. He's a wonderful man who allowed us to live above the small bakery, providing little means to purchase ingredients. We saved what little we earned, and though the bakery closed, the pastor insisted we keep everything we gained. It was my mother's idea to repay the pastor for his kindness, believing his teachings of the Creator were blessing those with charitable hearts.

But my mother doesn't rest. She continues to speak, her frail body shivering among the folds of her blue cotton dress and ragged sheets.

She lifts a shaky hand, motioning to the side of her small room. "Bring me my powder tin."

Without question, I go to the table. I keep my sights upon her, fearing if I look away, she will take her last breath, leaving me all alone. I lift the green tin with both hands.

"I always tried to take care of you. I did everything I could to assure you were safe and well."

Motioning, she reaches for the tin, her lips parting like a ripped seam on a doll. She wasn't always like this. In her youthful days, my mother was a vibrant woman, full of life and imagination. She always managed to create a story to explain away all the horrible things in the world. Her way of viewing the world never denied the fact of its darkness, but she always expressed a sense of hope amid the chaos.

All my life she tried to see the bright side, finding the

good in people and never once complaining out loud about our circumstances. She sang as she worked. She helped those less fortunate than us and comforted others who stood on the brink of ending it all. And though she never knew it. I would hear her cry herself to sleep every night whenever we went without pay or shelter or food for the day.

The box quakes in her frail hands as she tries to open the lid. I take the box and open it for her.

At first, I expect to see powder, a brush for her face, and maybe a comb for her hair, but the tin is filled with something more valuable.

"I always dreamed we'd board the train and travel to Oxlin to see the ocean. We'd find a cottage and live as we pleased, breathing the fresh air and feeling the beautiful freedom."

I lift thin blue papers, noting the fine printed designs showcasing their great value, and count them. There's enough money here for much more than a train ride.

I'm overcome and speechless. There were two more wads of folded papers, each a different color to portray their greater values. My trembling fingers brush the valuable red and green slips.

"Whenever times were the hardest, I held onto the dream of seeing the ocean. So many times, I wanted us to leave this place of soot and filth. But with all dreams we must wake to find ourselves in the noise and pain of reality."

I continue searching the contents of the tin, finding dried up flower petals. Whenever she picked a flower, she kept one petal for herself. It was something my mother always did. She'd always say, "If flowers were money, I'd keep just a bit. I'd save up all my petals and be happy and rich." There are so many petals, their vibrant colors are now blackened with time.

Tears pool along my eyelids. "I always wondered why you kept this tin. I assumed the powder eventually ran out and what remained was for sentimental purposes."

Our eyes meet, her cheeks wrinkling at the sides of her face as she tries to chuckle. "Indeed it was, my dearest son. Please listen, for I want you to know how grateful I am for you. You have been a strength and blessing to me . . . but now you must tend to yourself. When your father died, leaving us in ruin, you did your best to become a man. You did what you could to protect me. These past three years have been most difficult for you. I'm sorry I couldn't provide the life you were so deserving of."

I want her to stop talking. I don't want to hear it. I replace the lid upon the tin and wipe away my tears. I don't want to hear it. I can't. She can't be saying goodbye. Not now, not ever. With the money I could summon a doctor, someone who could give her the proper medicine she needs. I could take her out to the countryside, to Hallsent or Delova, where the fresh air could clear her dirty lungs.

There is so much I can do to help her. To keep her with me.

Her hand rests upon mine. I barely feel it. "You are a man now, my dearest Devin, and you are ready to stop tending to me. I free you of this burden placed upon you for so many years. You must go upon your own path. Go to Oxlin. See the ocean and feel the winds of freedom. Leave this place of filth and darkness. Fall in love and be happy with your choice."

I shake my head. "I don't know if I can. I don't know if I want to."

She uses what strength she has to grip my fingers. Her breaths quicken, and she attempts to lift her head. "If you do not leave this wretched place, then everything I have sacrificed, everything I have done to assure your safety and happiness, will be . . . for . . . nothing."

She pushes the tin close to my body and takes a few more deep breaths.

"Follow the example I have set for you. Do all you can to survive this cruel and unfair world. Promise me . . . you will."

Through sniffles, I nod. "I will. I promise."

But now, seeing her gaze empty and distant, I find myself truly alone.

CHAPTER 18

As the image of my dying mother fades into a sullen void, my body begins to awaken. I first notice the sound of a woman calling my name. She pats my face, hoping I will wake up. The sensation of her hand touching my cheek prompts my eyes to flutter beneath my eyelids.

Gradually my body wakes from its drug-induced sleep. It sounds strange, but I'm not sure if I am lying on my back or standing on my feet. I remember falling to the floor, calling to Selene as she cried.

I run my hands against whatever is behind me. I'm not in the grand lobby anymore. Instead of cold marble against my fingertips, I touch the rough, grainy veins of a wooden floor. My eyelids are still heavy, and I'm starting to recognize Sophia's voice.

"Mr. Foster, please wake. The servants . . . something is attacking them. Please, wake."

My fingers continue their journey, finding the fringe of

a floor rug. It's coarse. The smell of old books and lingering wood polish fills my nostrils. I'm in the library. I turn my head slowly, feeling every muscle in my neck stretch. My whole body aches as it revives, waking from its forced slumber. Slowly, I gain mobility in my legs and arms. I move them freely but not without concentration and meaningful effort.

A distant cry is heard, followed by a deep crash.

I try to lift my eyelids. The thin skin should be easy to peel away, but they hardly move.

"He's coming to," Sophia says, her tone filling with excitement.

I hear Diane's voice in the distance, reminding her to keep her voice down.

Another chorus of screams is clearly heard. I sense we're in danger, but I'm numb to the threat.

Slowly, my eyes blink open, revealing blurry patches of black and gray. I suspect the light grays are the moon's light. I swallow, but my throat is dry.

Rising to my elbows, I blink through dull patches of white and blue now filling my vision.

"Mr. Foster . . ." Sophia says, her face coming into focus. "Thank the Creator, you're awake."

I shake my head, still feeling a little disoriented. My arms and legs can move freely now.

"My head is pounding," Keagan says. "What in the Deep Abyss did they put in our drinks?"

I am sitting in the center of the library, surrounded by comfy armchairs and a footrest. Moonlight cascades through the windows, spilling over the deep, padded reading nooks at each window.

"Can you stand?" Sophia asks.

My vision comes into focus, and the woman stands over me, still in her blue evening gown. The blue sequins reflect the moon's light, giving her the appearance of a jeweled beacon. Her dark hair has fallen to her shoulders, and her eye makeup is smeared down her cheeks.

I nod my response.

"Remind me never to accept wine from a footman ever again," Keagan says with irritation. He props himself against a reading nook, rubbing his temples and stretching his back.

"We shouldn't be here," Diane says, pacing around the stairs which lead to the reading balcony. "This is all wrong. Marcus said we would wake at the circle of stones. Something's not right."

I watch the three worried people, my head spinning a little. "Where's Jerome?" I ask. My voice is breathy and strained.

Another yell, crash, and thud echo from the entrance leading to the servant quarters.

Diane stands behind me, nervously fiddling with her loose curls. Her small heels click on the wood floor. Facing me as she wrings her hands, the beautiful blonde speaks with a shrill voice. "Perhaps he's with the family at the circle of stones. Marcus told me Jerome might be with them because he'd already been through all this once before."

"Been through what?" Keagan questions.

Diane gives him a scathing look. "The Culling, Mr. Bottrell. We're in what is called the Culling. It's a horrible tradition, but it happens every time an Addington is engaged."

Keagan expresses his disgust. "I don't remember this happening when Elara and I got engaged."

Diane shrugs. "It's happening now. Marcus told me everything about it before we started courting. We weren't sure it would happen. Mr. Addington has acted less traditional these past years, and Marcus believed his father would allow us to live in peace. Then he overheard a conversation between his father and Uncle Alfred." She shudders and inspects the two entrances to the library. Both doors are wide open. One leads to the servant quarters and the other into the hallway.

"Had Quintin mentioned this, I would have never pressed him to come," Sophia says, cradling herself as she fights her tears. "I wanted him to ask for a humble allowance. Quintin is a skilled carpenter, and he means well, but . . ." She cradles her lower stomach and starts to hyperventilate. "Our unborn child needs more than what we can provide. Quintin doesn't know yet. I wanted to make sure we were established financially and then share the good news with him . . . but if I'm in danger . . ."

Diane embraces Sophia, muffling her growing sobs. "I won't allow you to be in peril. The Culling is a family tradition. A way to prove one's worth to the Addingtons. Fiancés and potential mates are forced to participate, but you're already a wife. Everything is all wrong."

I push myself to a stand but carefully lean against an armchair. "Because she's not wanted. I overheard Mrs. Addington telling a neighbor how Quintin was going to leave Sophia."

The woman begins to wail. "Is it true?" she asks me.

Shaking my head, I try to calm her. "He seems to love you very much. I don't think Eliza expects you or any of us to live. But this isn't who Arthur is. Perhaps it was Alfred who decided upon all this."

Another crash echoes, this time much closer.

Sophia again cradles her stomach. "I don't want to die. We shouldn't have come."

Diane clasps Sophia's shoulders, staring deep into her eyes. "Marcus told me how we must survive the night either by killing the Stalker or hiding until the Culling ends at sunrise. Marcus created a secret cellar in the gallery. He made the bars with silver—it's what the Stalker is vulnerable to. It burns through its skin as if it is as hot as the sun. It will keep us safe, but not all of us will fit. I fear the Stalker is near, judging by the sounds of trouble."

I recall the secret cellar in the gallery. The deep space behind the silver bars will only fit two adults. If the women take shelter there, Keagan and I can hide on the roof.

Keagan finds his balance and searches the room. "Where are the Addingtons?"

Diane shrugs. "Probably at the circle of stones. It's where we should have woken up. I don't know why things are different, but we must hide right now."

A loud scream echoes from the servant quarters. Everyone in the library is startled. Sophia screams but covers her mouth to muffle the sound. More screams now slice through the darkness, accompanied by a deep bellowing roar.

Keagan and I exchange glances. We both recognize the terrifying sound.

"It's the man beast," he breathes. He starts to panic as he searches for a place to hide.

My body stiffens as my heart races. I, too, search for a hiding place.

Softly, I touch Diane's shoulder. "You and Sophia can go to the gallery. If you run now, you should be able to make it."

More screams and shouts echo, turning our heads toward the doorway leading to the servant quarters.

"It's attacking the servants," Diane says, her chin trembling. She grabs Sophia's hand. "Come with me to the gallery."

Sophia takes a deep breath, overcome with fear. "Why didn't I know about this? Had I known, we wouldn't have come."

Diane swallows hard. "Perhaps he never intended to attend another one. Marcus told me Quintin left five years ago after his dearest fiancée, Maggie, was killed during the Culling. He demanded his father put an end to such a tradition, but Arthur would have been killed for his interference. Quintin couldn't be part of this family while the innocent died, all in the name of tradition."

A cry for mercy comes from the hallway on the other side of the wall.

Keagan throws his hands up in the air. "Why are we standing around waiting for this creature to kill us?" He stands to his feet as fast as he can. He staggers a little but starts making his way to the entrance leading into the hall.

"No," I say. "The women will go to the gallery. I know

another—"

A terrified servant dashes into the room. I recognize him to be a chimney sweeper named Benjamin. He's covered in blood and is hysterical as his body quivers. He pauses and stares at me, panting with confusion.

"It's in the house. It's forbidden to be in the house. Mr. Brent is helping the others to safety. He was going to return through the back door." Benjamin speaks quickly, frantically. "Mr. Addington said we'd be safe as always. Why are you standing there? You must—"

With a horrifying scream, the servant is yanked into the dark hallway by a large, clawed hand. His muffled screams are silenced, and only the sound of a deep growl is heard from the darkness.

Diane holds her breath. "We're too late."

Diane takes Sophia by the hand and pulls her up the small stairs to the reading balcony. They duck into the shadows.

Keagan is already tucking himself into a nearby closet beneath the stairs, pulling out the cleaning supplies in order to stuff his portly girth inside.

I freeze with panic. There's no place to hide. I'm completely out in the open.

More screams fill the hallway.

I observe the open door. My imagination runs wild, picturing the cursed man beast stepping through the doorway and reaching for me with his human-like hands. I can barely breathe. My body trembles as a deafening silence now fills the air. I hear footsteps coming toward the library. Why can't I move?

The familiar low growl echoes all around me. I force my legs to move, leaping into the nearest reading nook and pressing my back against the side, out of sight of the beast. My body freezes as the floorboards creak beneath the creature's heavy weight. I am too afraid to peek around the corner, but I am certain the monster stands in the doorway just beyond my view.

I hold my breath, pressing the palms of my hands against

the wall behind me. The loud sniff sends chills down my spine as the creature tries to catch our scent. Every muscle in my body tenses. I squeeze my eyelids shut and pray it won't find me.

I remain as silent and still as possible.

The beast continues to move farther into the room. It pushes aside an armchair. The wooden feet scrape against the hardwood floor. Slowly, I peek over my shoulder and see my shadow in the bright moon's light. I bite my lip to keep myself from gasping.

The creature continues moving forward. From the corner of my eye, the tip of the beast's nose appears. He stands on his hind legs, like a man, his tail brushing against the floor. Henry is incredibly tall, about as tall as a doorframe. Of course, the last time I saw him, he was quite a distance from me.

The beast swallows and takes in a couple deep breaths, his nostrils flaring. I assume my fate is sealed. I'm sweating profusely, my natural stench luring the creature to me. But instead of the beast facing me and tearing me apart, he continues moving forward, sniffing his way toward the reading balcony.

Did he catch one of the women's scents?

Slowly, I move my chin over my shoulder, watching the creature keep his nose high. I can see it now, filling me with greater terror. Its massive body towers over me. It bears a muscular frame covered in thick black fur. Its bristled tail sweeps along the floor as the monster's long pointed ears perk up with each sniff. I remain still, praying the beast doesn't turn in my direction. I assume if I can see the creature, then it can see me as well.

The monster takes another sniff, its nose tilting toward me. My heart stops. This is it. I'm going to die now.

I am certain the creature sees me, but its head jerks away when a bookend is thrown from the darkness above. Everything happens so quickly.

Henry roars, thick tufts of fur bristle along his back and broad shoulders. He charges ahead, knocking over more furniture as he bounds toward the women.

Sophia screams as the monster enters the darkness. My body is stiff with fear, and I stare at the darkness, listening to Diane command Sophia despite the monster's threatening bellows. I can't see what's happening, but eventually I watch Diane and Sophia spring from the other side of the balcony and race down the staircase.

Diane says nothing, passing me with Sophia on their way out of the library into the main hallway.

I glimpse the beast leaping from the balcony. I huddle in a small ball against the window. From my knees I watch Henry race out of the room and into the hallway, bounding after the women.

CHAPTER 19

I don't think the monster will come back. We should remain here, hiding in the shadows," Keagan says as he climbs out of his hiding place. He squeezes his mass from the smaller closet, stepping on toppled books and knocking over a few more. I'd never been more frightened of a falling object than I am at this moment. Any sound could attract the creature's attention.

"According to Diane, the Stalker is intended to kill us," I say. "Once he's finished downstairs, he'll search for us until he's succeeded."

Shaking his head as he carefully steps over the cleaning supplies, Keagan moves toward an armchair and sighs.

"I never thought the story was real," he says, peering over a mangled hand resting at the doorway. "I thought Elara was being odd."

I carefully inch my way out of the padded book nook. "You mean she told you everything?"

Mr. Bottrell shakes his head and rubs his face with both

hands. "Nothing about the Culling or man beasts. Only the angry, drunk human version of Henry."

The dead boy, Benjamin, lies in the doorway leading to the servant quarters, his blood inching its way into the spaces between the wooden slats. In the dim light, it's like a black puddle of oil, slowly coalescing, spilling over the threshold and finding the rug.

Keagan stretches his back, his body popping and cracking with each twist and turn. He's in shock, appearing unfazed by the dreaded situation we are in. He's sober now, but his cheeks are flushed with heat, and his hands tremble when placed at his sides.

"Well, since we can't follow the women to the secret cellar, and you're opposed to remaining here, perhaps we should get going to your secret hiding place. I assume there's room for the both of us." Keagan motions for me to lead the way out of the library. "Take me to it. If all we must do is wait until the sun rises, I hope we can do it safely wherever you intend us to go."

Nodding, I stand and walk toward the entrance leading into the hall. I listen for screams or cries to indicate the monster's location, but there's nothing. The house is filled with silence.

"There's a secret passage from the recreation room," I say. "It leads to the roof. I don't believe Henry will think to look for us up there."

My thoughts turn to Selene and our little adventure earlier today. Could she have known this would happen? Was she telling me something? Showing me a way out?

Maybe she didn't know anything about how tonight would play out. Diane said we were expected to start at the circle of stones, not inside the house.

Clearing his throat, Keagan motions again for me to lead the way. "Though I'm terrified of heights, being torn to shreds seems like a worse way to die," he says.

"Agreed."

We carefully make our way through the library, stepping

lightly as we go.

I reach the doorway leading into the main hallway and pause to make sure our path is safe. Filtered light fills the wide hallway, shrouding plants and other décor in half shadows. The air is thick with humidity, and the breeze outside has picked up to a whistling gale. My heart beats in time with the echo of the grand clock beside Mr. Addington's study.

"What of it?" Keagan whispers, his eyes as wide as saucers. "Are we safe to move?"

I hold my breath, taking another step, my heart pounding in my chest. I crane my neck from side to side, seeing no evidence of the creature. My eyes search the wide spaces of shadow, seeking any red glowing eyes.

The unnatural red eyes. The sharp teeth. Selene's painting is practically a portrait of Henry, not some creative interpretation.

"It's safe," I say, barely allowing my voice to escape my lips.

Keagan proceeds to follow me, but as I step into the hallway, I stop when a faint cry catches my attention. It's not a cry of fear. I listen carefully in order to locate where it's coming from. Keagan hears it as well and faces the servant quarters.

"Don't think about it," he says, blocking the doorway. "We need to get to the roof."

The voice speaks again, this time, clearer. It's a man's raspy voice, deep and filled with pain. "Please, help me. Anyone . . . help, me. Dearest Creator, have mercy upon me, I beg of thee."

I push Keagan aside, returning to the library, but he takes hold of my arm. "What do you think you're doing?"

"We should help him . . . bring him with us."

Keagan shakes his head, tightening his grip on me. "And what if he's past helping? His cries will only call the creature back to us."

"We can't leave anyone behind to die."

Keagan begins to shake. "I don't like it. Not one bit."

"Despite whether you like it or not, you can't gain access to the roof without me, so either wait here or join me.”

I stare at him as he contemplates the options. He taps his hands against his sides as his reluctance shifts into a resolution.

“Lead the way,” he hesitantly says.

I step around a large puddle of blood and enter the dark hallway.

Under the direction of Arthur four years ago, the current servant quarters were created to accommodate the house servants. He wanted to show greater respect for those who maintained his home. Each room was doubled in length to accommodate four bunk beds, a wardrobe, and a dresser. The grounds servants and gardeners live in similar quarters built behind the hedge maze.

The moment I step into the hallway, I brace myself against an end table, horrified at the carnage before me. Keagan gasps, covering his mouth.

From the adjacent hall, the moon’s light reveals the deathly wake of Henry’s wrath.

Before us is a row of doors, decorative plants placed between each one. Every door broken open, and some are blocked by a turned over bed. I recognize a body in the shadows, strewed about like a rag doll.

“Help me,” the pain-filled voice cries once again. It echoes from around the corner.

I take in a deep breath, detecting the copper stench of blood.

Pressing his back against the doorway, Keagan motions for me to continue.

We journey onward, peeking into each room as we pass them. The first five rooms are empty, untouched. Mr. Brent must have evacuated them before Henry started attacking.

I carefully step around two bodies crumpled against the wall. Dark blood oozes out of large slashes in their skin, staining their nightclothes and pooling onto the rug.

“I suggest you keep your gaze upon the window,” I say to Keagan. The halls in this area are covered in long rugs, muffling our steps.

"Help me," the man calls. "Please."

Up ahead the furniture is tossed about. Several shards of porcelain and marble litter the floor, and the thick curtains are torn down. As we turn the corner into the adjoining corridor, I withdraw for a second to compose myself.

The moon's light floods in through four large windows, bathing everything in a dull gray. Wispy clouds trail across the sky, partially obscuring the moon. The hall darkens momentarily as a large cloud passes. I breathe to steady my racing heart.

There are many more bodies down this hallway. Of the four bedrooms, three of the doors are broken to splinters, the last door ripped from its hinges.

"We can always turn back. I won't ever say you didn't try," Keagan whispers, keeping his eyes to the floor.

"I'm not giving up." I stay close to the wall, inching forward steadily.

Keagan grabs me and spins me to face him, pressing his thick thumbs into my shoulders. "This servant isn't worth it. None of them are. And if you sincerely wish to increase your status, you must understand there must be a balance, a requirement of others to suffer to assure we do not. Clearly the Addingtons have no care for their servants, as they've allowed a monster to rake through them like a pile of dead leaves."

Memories of my time in Linford working alongside my mother flood my mind. Constantly caught between the soot raining down from the tall smokestacks, and grime puddling at my feet, I'd watch the wealthy people with their clean, pressed suits and intricate parasols enter their carriages, laughing about meaningless things. They took no notice of me. Arthur Addington is nothing like them.

"Even if Arthur did think his servants dispensable, that need not be my attitude. But he happens to care a great deal about his servants. So much so, he moved them here."

"Then why did he allow them to be attacked?"

"Arthur wouldn't allow such a thing to happen. I refuse

to accept he is upholding the Culling. Perhaps his resistance has unintentionally caused these changes like us waking in the library and the Stalker entering the manor."

I pull away from Keagan and carry on through the horrible scene. Blood is splattered everywhere, clinging to the wallpaper, dripping down the windowpanes, and soaking the floor. Mr. Brent wasn't able to warn this corridor in time.

I avoid searching rooms as I listen for the voice to call out again.

Keagan reluctantly follows, keeping in pace as I step around the broken bodies.

We're now at the back of the house. A line of windows with curtains pulled closed allows little moonlight into the corridor. The end of this narrow hallway leads back into the main hall. There are five more bedrooms, their doors smashed open, and each of them is dark and silent.

"Is someone . . . there? Please . . . Mr. Brent, I'm here," the servant calls much louder.

Keagan and I rush toward the room. I pull open the nearest set of curtains, allowing light to fill the hallway. I don't know what to expect, I'm prepared to carry the injured servant to the recreation room and up the stairs to the roof. I wipe my sweaty forehead with the back of my sleeve and step over the threshold.

"We're here," I whisper loudly.

At the back of the room, leaning against a bunk bed, a man stares at me.

Most of the furniture is tossed about like toys in a playroom. One servant is dead at my feet, his body in a heap beside a broken dresser. Another is pinned against the wall.

"Mr. Brent . . . are you there?" the surviving man says. "Please, help me."

I gingerly make my way toward him. "Rodney," I say, climbing over the toppled wardrobe and reach for him. I pause when I realize he's not happy to see me.

"Mr. Foster," Rodney says, his dull gray eyes blinking

slowly. "You mustn't be here. I'm not allowed to speak with you. We can't interfere once the Culling has begun."

"It doesn't matter. We've come to help you." When I finally make it to his side, I take a closer look at Rodney's condition, looking him over from head to foot.

The old man's body is badly torn and still bleeding. In the pale light, he's as white as the sheets upon the bed. He sees the hopelessness in my eyes and reaches for me.

He's lost too much blood. "I'm so sorry," I whisper, taking his hand in mine.

The servant leans his head against the wall. "If the man be enraged, then the beast be as well. If the man be . . . enraged." He takes quicker breaths, turning his gaze to the darkness surrounding us. "A foul temper feeds the beast. He should have left us all alone, but an evil man will do evil deeds."

Keagan shakes his head, wagging a finger at the servant. "The man is delirious. He speaks in riddles."

"He wasn't allowed within the home," Rodney says. He tries to move away from me, pulling his hand from my grasp and pressing his body against the nearest wall. His eyes dart wildly throughout the room as if he's caught in a terrible dream. "They allowed him inside. We were supposed to be safe here. Master Addington always assured us of our safety."

"What changed this time?" I ask.

"Mr. Brent told us to clear out and go to the hedge maze. He said Mr. Addington told us to, but none of us believed him. The house is forbidden to the Stalker. We're supposed to be safe here."

I try to calm the man. "Who is the Stalker?"

Rodney breaks down in tears and takes quick breaths. He stares into the darkness and digs his fingers against the wooden floor. "Wasn't allowed to come here."

Keagan is upset and turns away from the dying servant. "We're wasting time. We need to get to the roof."

When I face Rodney, his eyes stare blankly. No breath

escapes him. He's gone.

I sit in silence, thinking about his words. The connection of a man's rage to the beast's bloodlust is perplexing.

"Why is all this happening?" I ask, more to myself than to Keagan. A deep aggravation grows within me. I rub my hands over my face and try to calm myself. I must keep my wits about me.

Henry is well known for his bad temper. Perhaps he's blinded by his bloodlust, incapable of deciphering the difference between servant and chosen prey for the Culling. I wouldn't think a monster to have a sound mind or conscience, but if this monster is half man, surely there's some humanity within him.

Why didn't Selene follow Marcus's example and warn me? None of this makes sense, but what does it matter? The Culling is happening now. I'm in danger now.

"When the morning sun comes, I will most certainly call off my engagement," Keagan says. "This is insane. I expect some answers."

"I agree, but . . ." I sigh.

"But what?" Keagan asks. He motions to Rodney and the upset room. "Don't you feel betrayed?"

"Of course I do!" I say, remembering to keep my voice low. "But I'm refusing to allow such thoughts of opposition to overcome me. I want to believe Arthur is a good man. I want to believe Selene loves me, despite whatever obstacles stand between us. If I allow even an ounce of doubt to enter my mind, I fear I won't make it through the night. I'm terrified, Keagan, and I'm already tired of just surviving."

A heavy feeling lifts from my chest. I stare at the dandy and his velvet trousers and golden buckles.

"I may never have the fancy house or beautiful wife. Life has always been a struggle for me, but I cannot allow everything to weigh me down. I, too, need answers. I can't give up. I'd like to believe there is something worth fighting for tonight. Arthur wouldn't have allowed this, and I choose to hold true to such a belief. I can choose to despise those who didn't prevent me from being part of this, or I can try to understand their reasons. This is all a misunderstanding—it has to be—I have to believe it is. We'll wait out the night upon the roof and hopefully get to the bottom of all this in the morning."

Keagan lets out a long sigh and presses his shoulders against the wall. "And here I thought something was wrong with you mentally. Turns out your emotions have gone awry."

Keagan places a heavy hand upon my shoulder. "It's unfortunate about the servant. You can't save them all. Obviously, Mr. Brent can't either."

I brush aside his hand, feeling agitated.

Keagan walks toward the doorway. "Well, c'mon, Devin," he says sullenly. "We need to get to the roof. You can mourn for the needy later."

CHAPTER 20

Iinspect the empty grand hallway. The wind howls outside the windows as the moon's light dims behind developing clouds. Keagan and I exchange one last moment of second-guessing our actions, and I ball my trembling hands into tight fists. I wish I knew exactly where Henry is, but I'm also relieved the house is silent. Keagan's heavy breaths fan against the back of my neck, the only perceptible sound.

There are two grand hallways in Addington Manor. The main level, which feeds into the ballroom, gallery, drawing room, and kitchen. And then we have this second-level grand hallway. It isn't as wide, since there are more bedrooms upstairs to encroach upon the space, but it's still filled with decorative furnishings such as polished end tables, heavy statues, and intricate vases. Unfortunately, this grand hallways lacks any covering over the wooden floor.

I fear every step will announce our location, drawing the beast toward us. Without words, I remove my shoes, holding them with one hand, encouraging Keagan to do the same. Though the weight of our bodies won't stop the floor from creaking, at least the lack of shoes will prevent any additional noise.

"We have to pass the first hall and turn left at the next," I say, motioning to our destination.

"Why does the hall appear so much longer now?" Keagan whispers.

Ignoring him, I take my first step. My socks are sweaty, stunting any chance of slipping. The floor releases a steady creak. My blood pulses through my temples.

"Go on," Keagan urges, gripping his shoes tightly in his hands.

Never has such a simple thing inspired so much fear. I make my way across the hall, keeping the sides of my feet pressed against the baseboards where the floor is less likely to groan under my weight. Keagan does the same, but his feet create a chorus of thumps, and thuds. He's like an elephant at a table set for a tea party, trying his best to be dainty but failing miserably.

I wedge myself between an end table and potted plant. As Keagan joins me, he clumsily knocks over a vase. I lunge forward and catch it with my free hand inches from the floor. I have half a mind to break it over his head.

"Unbelievable," I whisper and give him a sour look.

He sheepishly smiles as if to apologize in silence. I look for a safe place to put the vase down.

Suddenly we're both startled by a loud bang of pots and pans coming from directly below us. Amid the surprise, the vase slips from my hand and breaks into several pieces at my feet.

Keagan lets out an audible gasp as I panic and swallow hard.

I stare at the fragments in horror. "Run," I say, the word bursting from my throat.

Wild screams are heard coming from the kitchen. More clangs and bangs follow as a man is heard yelling his final cries. A woman screams for help before another loud bang echoes through the manor.

Slipping on his shoes, Keagan steps around the broken vase and dashes, every step he makes is like a cannon blast.

I'm but a breath behind him, replacing my shoes and dashing toward the end of the grand hallway. My blood runs cold as it races through my veins. I don't look away from the stairs as I run, both fearing what I will see ascending them and unwilling to be caught by surprise.

The tips of black ears appear first, followed by the broad brow atop two glowing, red eyes. He's found us. My whole body shudders at the sight.

Keagan sees it too and runs faster, widening the distance between us. He's already turning the corner, but I'm not as lucky.

The beast gives out a shattering roar, blood dripping from his jowls and long black claws. He stands on two legs like a man, steadily moving, his eyes fixed on me. He watches me run, calculating my route and planning his assault. He lunges as I near the corner, but his long claws slip on the bare wooden floor, and he loses his balance.

I rush into the recreation room and slam the door shut, yelling to Keagan to help me create a barricade with the heavy furniture.

But instead of complying to my demand, Keagan stares at me, his eyebrows pinched together with concern. He points to the floor.

Huddled behind the sofa are three children. Hattie is the young maidservant who tends to Selene. She clings to Ingrid and Thomas, who hide their faces at Hattie's side. She stares at Keagan as she fights back tears.

"Is Mr. Brent on his way to save us?" she asks, her voice trembling with fear.

Keagan looks at me, not knowing what to say.

The grisly growls and powerful bangs against the door make the children scream.

"Help me, Keagan!" I yell, breaking his distracted trance. "I can't hold the door for long. Hattie, I need your help as well."

Little Thomas begs her not to move. She shakes her head, tears now falling from her eyes.

"I'm sorry."

Defeated, I understand. "It's fine. Keep him quiet."

Keagan pushes a nearby dresser toward me, his bulk finally being useful for once. As I help him finish the dresser's journey, Henry pierces the thick wood door with his claws. With the dresser secured, Keagan pushes the heavy sofa toward me, his face now a beet red. I hesitate to help him, certain I should support the dresser in order to hold back the Stalker once he breaks through the door.

I don't think Keagan has ever exerted himself this much his entire life.

"Mr. Brent said he'll return to us," Hattie says. "Where is he?"

I face her, pressing my back against the dresser and planting my feet. "He's probably on his way, but Mr. Bottrell and I are here to help now. Take the children and go to the far wall. There's a button in one of the wooden planks that opens a secret room. Go find it."

Hattie shakes her head, sobbing. "I'm afraid."

"You have to do this! Please! I will hold back the beast, but you must move quickly."

"If we interfere, the Guardian will kill us."

Stalker? Now a Guardian? What is it guarding?

The sofa presses against the dresser, and I step away. Rodney also said the servants couldn't interfere. Does this apply to family members as well? Would this Guardian kill Arthur and Selene if they interfered? Perhaps this massacre is punishment for that interference.

"Hattie," I say, crouching to look directly in her eyes. "You're not interfering. You're saving yourself and these two children. If anything, I'm the one interfering on your behalf."

"It's in the rules," she says, her tear-stained face full of confliction.

"It's also in the rules that the Stalker is not allowed in the manor. Please, forget about the rules and try to survive."

Hattie swallows hard and nods. I help her to her feet, and she takes the two children by the hand and follows me to the far wall. I try to remember exactly where Selene stood when she unlocked the secret door.

Keagan runs to the window and tries to push it open. He lets out an angry cry and hits the glass with his hand.

"It won't open. We're trapped. There's no way to the roof," Keagan says.

At the door, fragments of wood break free. The glaring red eyes peer through the narrow hole.

My fingers search the planks of wood and find the button. Without hesitation, I press it.

The seam in the wall gives way, and I pull open the door, motioning for everyone to enter.

Keagan races past me, ignoring the children who do their best to hurry while crying and holding onto Hattie.

Once the children have entered the secret hallway, I step inside, giving one last glance at the monster at the door, his red eyes narrowing at his failure to get to us.

CHAPTER 21

Securing the door, I listen to the loud bangs coming from Henry as he tries to break into the recreation room. Loud, menacing roars find their way to me, making my skin crawl.

I dash up the stairs, following Keagan into the room.

"What are we going to do?" he says, pacing. "We're trapped. The monster will break through any minute now."

Hattie and the children huddle together in the far corner, Thomas is sobbing. Every echoing bang from the stairs below makes him jump. Ingrid remains quiet, grasping tightly to Hattie and hiding her face.

I must keep them alive, but I'm not sure how to do it.

We can't stay here. Rodney said Mr. Brent ordered the servants to the hedge maze, so perhaps we'd all be safe there. We could escape the manor by leaping to the tree, but I don't know if Hattie or the children could make the jump. They'll never outrun the beast.

If Keagan and I somehow lure him away from the children

and keep him distracted, perhaps he'll forget about them.

Keagan looks around the room, turning his nose at the heavy scent of dust and mildew. "What do you propose we do?"

And like the light sparking from a match, the idea comes to me.

In the library the beast was following Diane and Sophia's scents. Perhaps I can use the stench of this room to our advantage.

I run to the nearest armchair and desk, pulling off the old sheets. I demand Keagan do the same with the remaining furniture.

The wooden sofa feet scrape against the floor in the recreation room, screeching loudly as the monster breaks through. This causes Ingrid to scream and cry harder into Hattie's side. The maidservant stares at me with desperate eyes. Her long blonde locks cascade over her shoulders as she attempts to stop trembling.

I place a soft hand upon Thomas and Ingrid, trying to calm them.

"Nothing is going to happen to you. I promise it. It's all right."

Ingrid looks at me with puffy eyes, her small, pouted lips quivering. "The monster is going to eat us."

I shake my head. "No, he's not. He's not going to hurt you because we're going to play a little game. Are you familiar with hide and seek?"

Another loud screech echoes from the room. Thomas looks toward the stairs, his hands shaking. "Please, don't let him get me," he says, steadying his breath.

I lean into his sight, our eyes meeting as I touch his soft blond hair. "I won't allow it. I want you to take Hattie and Ingrid and hide beneath the bed. Cover yourselves with these sheets."

His dark brown eyes check the bed. It's like a box, its bedframe reaching the floor. I wrap the sheet around the boy.

A forceful bang comes from the base of the stairs. The three children scream and cry, but I motion for them to gather closer to me.

"No screaming. You must fight the urge," I say over the constant pounding and scratching.

Henry continues to fight his way through the plaster and wood concealing the secret door. He must have followed our scents.

Keagan hands me a few sheets, and I wrap Hattie and Ingrid inside them. I remain calm and speak steadily. "The beast can smell all sorts of things, but when you are shrouded in this sheet of invisibility, not only will the beast not be able to see you, but he won't smell you either."

Thomas sniffles. "You're not telling the truth. He'll find us. He'll find us, and he'll eat us."

I motion to their hiding place. "Not if you're underneath the bed. His nose guides him. If you smell like a pile of dusty bedsheets, he'll assume you're a pile of dusty bedsheets."

Keagan helps lift the heavy bed frame. There's enough room beneath it for the children to slip into the shallow crevice and huddle close to each other. I add an extra sheet to all three of them once I've helped them inside the dark nook.

We carefully lower the bed, forcing the children to press their stomachs against the floor.

Peeking between the thin slats, I take a final glance at the pile of sheets hiding the frightened children. "You must remain silent. I'm going to attract the creature to me, so he won't care about you. As long as he's focused on me, he won't hurt you. I promise. Cup your hands across your mouths to make sure you don't make a sound."

The sheets shift as the children pull their hands over their mouths.

"Good. I must add a few more sheets to hide your scent. Do not come out until you see the sun's light through the sheets. Be brave and stay quiet. We don't want anyone to hear you until it's safe to come out. Do you understand?"

They each reply in the affirmative, their responses short as they fight to hold back the tears.

"Thank you," Hattie says, bravery shining through the quivers in her voice.

I cover the bed with additional sheets. Keagan helps, his attention never far from the base of the stairs. We don't have much time.

I grab his arm and dash to the double doors leading to the metal balcony.

"There's an oak tree growing near to the house. We'll jump to it and run to the hedge maze," I say, swinging open the doors and pushing him outside. I leave the doors wide open, signaling to the beast we've escaped.

Keagan considers this for a moment before accepting that this is our only option. "I pray Mr. Brent and the servants won't turn us away for fear of interfering, but first we must survive the leap."

A refreshing wave of wind washes over us, cooling my sweaty skin and clearing my chaotic thoughts.

I point to the ladder. "That way."

As Keagan makes his way down, I can hear the splintering of wood from within the room. Henry will tear through at any moment.

"Hurry!" Keagan yells.

But I can't go on. I'm frozen with fear, but surprisingly not at the beast or my impending leap from the roof. I'm terrified the children won't be able to hold in their screams, and the man beast will find them.

From the balcony, I inspect the platform below. The drop is not quite twice my height, but from there the far corner of the roof feels like it reaches all the way to the horizon. The large oak tree beyond holds its thick crown to the heavens. I motion for Keagan to start running, but I stand firm, determined to be the first thing Henry sees.

"Come on, Henry," I whisper, watching the stairs. "Come on."

A surge of energy burns in my muscles as I wait for the moment we lock eyes to jump to the platform. The beast must follow.

A few more thunderous pounds echo through the room. I stand ready, my whole body tense.

The wall gives way, and the man beast ascends the stairs in seconds, roaring at the top of his lungs.

A chorus of screams escapes from beneath the bed, but I yell louder, waving my hands about and calling for the monster to get me instead.

Keagan cries out for me to stop, but it's too late. Henry charges toward me.

I leap from the metal balcony, rolling carefully onto the platform as Henry bursts through the doorframe. He vaults into the air, his claws outstretched, his jaws wide open. Lightning rips through the clouds as he soars, highlighting his hulking figure. My eyes follow the beast as he lands on the shingles beside us.

"To the tree!" I yell, swiftly gaining on Keagan.

We race toward the edge of the roof, Henry swiping his massive hand but misses me by inches.

A distant grumble of thunder accompanies another slice of lightning. The moon's light seeps through breaks in the clouds, lighting our way along some divine path.

The beast jumps from peak to peak, shingles shedding beneath his weight. He stumbles and slips his way over the uneven terrain which has little to sink his claws into for purchase. I thank the Creator that this allows Keagan and me to move quicker than Henry.

We reach the point where Selene stood, and I gasp with disbelief.

There among the shuddering leaves is a platform. Wide, wooden planks are secured upon a thick branch and reach straight to the trunk. It's unbelievable. I'd never noticed it before.

"She wanted to show this to me," I breathe.

Keagan grabs my arm. "I don't think I can make it." The

wind whips his hair wildly around his face.

I watch Henry draw closer. "Have a little faith, dear man, or die by the hand of a devil."

I pull him away from the edge. We need a running start. Keagan hesitates, but I waste no time arguing.

I sprint, aware of the beast drawing near. Keagan yells as he, too, runs toward the tree.

I take a deep breath and leap into the night air.

CHAPTER 22

Crashing onto the platform, my body skids over the sturdy planks and is stopped by sharp branches. Keagan lands with a hard thud, and I serve as an unwilling buffer between him and the branches, bringing his momentum to a halt.

Flashes of lightning illuminate the leaves in shades of gray as the wind makes them shiver like a thousand sails caught in a squall. My body aches from the impact, but I'm grateful to still be alive. Keagan glances at me, standing and collecting himself as a smile stretches over his face. We exchange looks of unbelievable luck.

But our little victory is short-lived. Henry dives for the limb supporting the platform.

Henry's violent impact brings Keagan to his knees, and he stumbles over me as the man beast begins to draw near. The tree shakes viciously as Henry ducks and pushes through the wooded barrier. His claws cut and tear at the thicker branches with ease. He slinks his body between the hundreds of branches, releasing yips of discomfort along the way. The tree thrashes so violently I'm forced to remain on my knees.

The main branch supporting the platform starts to snap like brittle bushels of straw, echoing loud pops in my head. The stench of animal fur and broken wood fills the air. I keep close to the platform planks and crawl toward the trunk. I feel as though I am on a ship swaying in a turbulent sea.

The closer Henry gets to us, the more the branch gives way.

"This isn't going to be pleasant," Keagan says as he hugs himself and covers his face.

There's no time to react, no time to move. I watch in horror as the branch's joint snaps and splits away from the trunk.

Keagan and I fall beneath a wave of foliage. For a moment I'm shrouded in darkness, feeling a current of wind against my back. Henry lets out a terrible roar, and the three of us slam into the ground.

I come out of my stunned state and hear only silence. Cautiously, I push away branches and sharp twigs, finding a clearing in the tree's canopy above. I stare at the cloudy sky in an attempt to regain my bearings. The moon's light cuts through the haze in beams. Everything is blanketed in shades of gray light and shadow. I continue to brush away little twigs and leaves, noticing a tear in my jacket.

Earlier today I worried about maintaining the condition of my clothing. I fretted over the possibility of ripping through the delicate fabric, but I pay no heed to it now. Removing the jacket induces a sharp pain from my side. I carefully slip off the garment and toss it aside. For now, my well-fitted vest provides a little comfort as I search the mesh of leaves and wood for Keagan. We must get a head start to the hedge maze before Henry wakes up.

"Keagan?" I whisper, trying to shift some large branches to get a look underneath. I grasp my ribs, grimacing at the sharp jolt on my right side. Taking a deep breath, I push through the pain and distance myself from the pile of debris.

"Keagan?" I cry once again, still searching for him.

I'm met with silence. As I stand alone, a paralyzing thought enters my mind. I must go on without Keagan. Perhaps he didn't survive the fall, in which case there's nothing I can do for him. If he's alive and I stay and look for him, the beast will surely take us both. But if I go, at least one of us has a chance. Henry may chase after me, or he may prefer easier prey. I have no way of knowing.

Thunder grumbles closer to the manor, the air turning cold as the storm slowly moves more inland. I moan from the pain in my side but hurry away from the devastation.

I glance at the grand oak tree, startled by its missing limb. What once represented growth and patience is now maimed. Below it, Henry's dark shadow rises in the flickers of lightning. His low growl sends a deep chill racing down my spine.

The bare teeth and evil eyes of Henry Addington shine in the faint moonlight. A hate-filled threat reverberates from his throat, and his ears bend backward. He appears unscathed from the fall, though bits of leaves and twigs mingle with his black fur. He slowly approaches me on all fours, gnarring as his large hands and padded feet press into the soft ground.

"Please, don't do this," I say, holding out my hands. "I am no threat to the family. I beg you to have mercy upon me." My words pour from my lips and fall upon deaf ears. This beast is not a harbinger of compassion. Nothing about him expresses the hint of charity.

Thick tufts of fur rise on the back of his shoulders, giving him a more menacing appearance as he lurks closer. The moon's light extends his shadow over me. I'm not sure what's more unnerving, the thought of him instantly attacking and tearing me to pieces, or his slow creeping toward me. He circles around the tree, driving me closer to Addington Manor.

"Devin!" Keagan shouts, breaking free of the oak's fallen limb and tossing a few branches at the beast. He quickly grabs me and gains the lead. "To the hedge maze!"

I praise the Creator that Keagan is alive and seemingly well.

With the slight distraction, I follow Keagan, cradling my ribs with my left hand. Pushing myself to run, I welcome what little relief I have with this notion. All this time, Keagan is shouting and waving his arms madly, drawing the beast's attention toward him instead of me.

We run toward the hedge maze, refusing to look back. I stare at the tall parameter of boxwood shrubs, their height at least ten feet. Menacing walls of foliage tower over us, encasing us in darkness as we run around deep shadowy corners and through lengthy corridors.

Unsure of our direction, we don't know where exactly Mr. Brent was taking the servants, and the exertion of running is hindering both of us. With the beast's ability to track by scent, we're dependent on luck and miracles.

"I know a place where we can go," I say, guiding him around a few corners. "There's a hidden cellar on the other side of the maze." Selene and I would frequently go there for more privacy. "We'll head there, and if we're lucky we'll encounter the servants' hiding place."

Breathing heavily, Keagan asks no questions, but presses forward.

We turn a corner, entering a small opening displaying a statue of a tall beast. The dingy marbled creature startles us, making Keagan cry out.

I glance around to see if Henry is pursuing us, but all is quiet. Hope lights within me as I wonder if some magic keeps him away from the maze, but I can't let my guard down. Most likely Henry is prowling, preparing a final, deadly pounce.

"We're almost there," I say, motioning for Keagan to follow.

I study each turn, recalling the path leading us to the cellar. We move silently through the maze, Keagan keeping in step with me. The air is stale, trapped within the narrow pathways.

In the distance I can hear the fountain bubbling. It centers the maze, its white marble base carved with wolf heads. Blood lilies and daisies grow nearby. The memory of first visiting the fountain with Selene comes to mind, but I grasp my ribs tighter to focus my attention. Now isn't the time to recall fond memories of lingering glances, holding hands, and basking in the sun beside the woman I love. If anything, I must focus in order to see her once again, if I can.

Coming to an intersection, I pause, not recognizing the place. There should be a stone basin filled with a blue rosebush, but instead there are three other paths to take.

"Are you lost?" Keagan asks. He gratefully catches his breath but waves for me to continue.

I remain silent as I see the pair of red eyes staring directly at me from a distance to the left. Without hesitation this time, Henry charges, his wide shoulders brushing against the thick foliage, his massive hands reaching for me with each step.

I run across the intersection, away from the moon's light, making my way through the sharp corners and short corridors.

"Hurry, Keagan," I say, coming to another opening and getting my bearings back.

But Keagan doesn't respond. He's gone.

I hear rustling behind me and carry on. Perhaps Keagan took another path and is moving safely away from Henry. Now completely lost, I turn a sharp corner. Everything looks different through my fear. I follow a long corridor shrouded in darkness, reaching forward and steadily keeping my pace until I come to a wall. Like a blind man, I feel my way around the corner and enter another dimly lit clearing. Within the center of the space is a large marble box with dying flowers withering in its opening. I search frantically for another exit but realize I'm at a dead end.

Taking a moment to catch my breath, I search for other means of escape. I can't dig through the wall. It's at least three feet thick with tightly woven branches and a thatch fence creating the shape of the maze itself. I try climbing, removing my hand from my aching ribs in order to reach for a hold within the bushes. It's no use. I wince and pull away with pain.

My heart stops when I hear footsteps. Holding my breath, I

wait for Henry and accept my fate.

I move to the farthest corner and press myself into the branches, ignoring the sharp pokes against my body. In my final moments, I think of Selene and hold the image of her precious smile within my mind. I reflect over our first kiss, the long walks around the yard, and how beautiful she looks walking around the rose garden in spring.

The steps draw closer, and I brace for the worst.

"Mr. Foster," Mr. Brent says, "thank the Creator, you're still alive."

I stare at the old man who holds a small metal lantern in his hand. Instantly I'm relieved and filled with gratitude. I walk toward the flickering light and greet Mr. Brent with a respectful bow.

I speak rapidly, taking no time to breathe. "I don't know where Keagan is. We were separated. Please help us."

"We need to get you to the circle of stones," Mr. Brent says. "It's the only way to end all this."

"What about Keagan?"

A defeated look washes over his face. "Diane and Keagan will not be harmed this night. Only those who aren't selected to survive must prove themselves worthy of the family association. Is Sophia all right?"

I shrug, unsure if the women made it to Marcus's cellar, but my thoughts focus on Mr. Brent's words.

"Keagan and Diane? They won't be harmed?"

"No," he says, his brow knitted with tension. "The Stalker was commanded to kill only you and Sophia. You two were chosen as prey."

My breath catches in my throat. In the library, Henry wasn't going after both women. He was targeting Sophia. My thoughts turn to the servants. Why did they still have to die if only Sophia and I were selected as prey?

"So many are dead. So many servants."

A sullen look washes over Mr. Brent's face. "Casualties

of an unchecked bloodlust. Nothing is going according to plan tonight, and I don't know why."

Mr. Brent glances into the nearest corridor. "But I'm happy you were able to get out of the house. Everything is locked now at the manor. I wasn't able to gather more servants before the Culling officially started."

He motions for me to follow, but I remain still. "You knew all this time? You knew Keagan and I saw the beast at the circle of stones, and you denied it! You made me think I was foolish or insane."

The old man lowers his head in shame. "I swore with my life to always protect the Addington family and their secret. In my youth I spoke to Ms. Taylor thinking it would impress her, but obviously it only made her curious about the wealthy family. She began sharing what I told her, catching the attention of local hunters who believed her story. They threatened to murder the family if they didn't leave Anna's Cove. Brandon Addington, Arthur's father, was able to convince the men that Lydia was feebleminded and prone to fanciful tales. Eventually the hunters left the family in peace, but my life was on the line due to my neglect. I swore I would never speak of their secret ever again.

"As for Ms. Taylor, she was humiliated by Demora Addington when, for a season, she wasn't invited to any social gatherings hosted by her dear friend. This cost Lydia her reputation, and she was seen as an open gossiper. She left Anna's Cove, only to return, years later after the death of her husband. She's never forgotten the mistreatment of the Addingtons and still repeats my words to this day, but no one takes her seriously. Keagan and Diane still need to participate in the Culling so they know exactly what will come for them should they ever reveal the family's secret."

"Keeping the family's secret in exchange for their lives?" I ask.

Mr. Brent nods and nervously looks around.

The sting of reality pierces my soul, filling me with bitterness and a pain I've never felt before. Why didn't Selene tell me all this? Most importantly, why did Arthur order my execution?

"You shouldn't be interfering," I say with irritation.

"For almost fifty years, I've watched newly engaged fiancés fall prey to the vicious beast this family submits to. Let the Guardian take me so I might face my rightful judgment." Mr. Brent reaches from behind his back and reveals a small revolver. "You're like a son to Arthur. He admires your kind heart, and I share his sentiment. Within this family, men grow bitter, and their hearts harden, but not Arthur's. You remind him of his freedom from the burdensome expectations which come with his family name. It's why he chose you."

"Chose me to die?"

His face hardens. "No, stupid boy, he chose you to live. He never intended this night to happen ever again, but the one who upholds the Culling mustn't be challenged. If there's resistance, the Guardian will stop it immediately—no matter who it is."

I take the gun, its ivory handle almost glistens in the light of the lantern. It's a Whistler, a weapon constructed ahead of its time. It has a short, single barrel, and multiple chambers within a revolving cylinder that can hold three lead balls. I've seen a few men in town using Whistlers for target practice and handled one myself a few times, but this particular weapon is different. It's metal frame shimmers like silver, and it's a little lighter in my hand.

Mr. Brent motions for us to leave, and I willingly comply. Tucking the gun within my belt, I try to keep up with the old man.

"At the circle of stones, there's an altar of weapons designated for the prey to select as defense against the Stalker." Mr. Brent explains, pointing to the gun in my hand. "This is the one you want. Arthur understood he wasn't' in control of the Culling, and you'd be left defenseless. He gave this gun to me as protection as I helped the servants get out. He also made me promise to transfer the gun to you or Sophia if such an opportunity arose.

I've done my duty, though I doubt Arthur has the authority to grant me such license to interfere."

"Is Alfred the one behind all this?" I ask.

Mr. Brent stops in his tracks and raises the lantern. Half his face is lit in bright orange light, giving him a sinister look.

"Alfred is the Guardian. He ensures the Culling will go on, and he has threatened Arthur with punishments worse than death should he continue to oppose it. When the Culling is finished, he will execute the suitable punishments for interference." Mr. Brent shudders at the thought of his own fate.

"I swear I'll never tell him."

Mr. Brent smirks and carries on walking. "He has his ways of finding things out."

"If Alfred isn't in charge, who else is there?"

I remember the final toast that began the Culling and reach my conclusions as Mr. Brent speaks the name. "Eliza Addington."

My breath catches in my throat.

So much is placed upon the mother to uphold the social reputation of the family. I suppose it makes sense why she would support this ritual. I almost want to laugh at my naïve thought this morning that Eliza's sour scowls were the worst thing I'd have to endure from her.

"She's waiting with the others at the circle of stones." Mr. Brent pauses to make sure we're safe, carefully peeking around a corner before looking me over. "But you'll need to kill the Stalker before you leave the hedge maze. Once he's out of the way, go to the family, tell them what you've done, and swear allegiance. It's the only way to be spared."

CHAPTER 23

"There are a few able men among the servants who can help us," Mr. Brent says. "If we lure the Stalker toward the center of the maze, we can provide a distraction, giving you opportunity to shoot him."

I can hear the water pouring in the distance. We're getting closer to the center fountain. Cautiously I look around, on high alert for any rustle announcing Henry's presence. He's surely prowling after me.

"I'm not good with a gun," I say timidly. "What if I miss?"

Mr. Brent glances over his shoulder, giving me a disappointed look. He opens his mouth to speak but stops in a moment of distraction.

"Stay quiet," he says. He looks ahead of the path as well as behind us.

The familiar nervous feeling returns, making my palms sweat. I tighten my grip on the gun so it won't slip.

"What is it?" I whisper.

Without warning, Henry's clawed hand punches through the shrubbery wall and grabs at my back, taking hold of my clothes.

The butler grabs me as I'm pulled into the thick foliage. Tiny twigs dig into my flesh, and I frantically try to wriggle free. Henry has a tight grip on my shirt and vest, his claws caught in the fabric. I tug at my vest buttons. If I can get it off, my shirt should rip away easily. The first button gives way, falling to my feet.

Mr. Brent grasps my shoulders, participating in a deadly game of tug-of-war. The beast roars, his grip remaining firm on the stiff material of my vest. My fingertips fumble with the last two buttons.

"Got it!" I say, slipping out of the garment. With a loud rip, the back of my shirt tears away and I'm free, stumbling forward into Mr. Brent.

The beast pulls my vest through the hedge wall. A wild roar bursts from his hiding place.

Mr. Brent and I race along another corridor, turning into the open space surrounding the fountain. Several servants huddle together, nervously looking at my cuts and scrapes.

"The Stalker is coming. We need to keep Mr. Foster safe," Mr. Brent says, commanding the women and children to quietly flee to another part of the maze.

Keagan steps out from among the servants, gawking at my appearance. "I'm so glad you weren't eaten. I ran away from the monster and stumbled upon this place," he says.

The butler ushers me to the fountain as he stares at the remaining men. "It won't be long until the beast finds us here. He's coming for his prey. We have a chance to help Mr. Addington stop this once and for all. If the prey kills the Stalker, they will no longer be able to uphold this wretched tradition. We must stand together. Mr. Foster is armed and ready. We only need to give him an opportunity to fire."

The men hesitate, each keeping their heads bowed, their shoulders slumped. I want to say something to them but before I can even open my mouth, everyone's attention is drawn upward as Henry vaults through the air, leaping over the tall hedge.

When the hulking beast lands upon the ground, he releases a threatening roar, causing everyone to distance themselves.

"Now is your chance," Mr. Brent shouts.

I raise my trembling hand and squeeze the trigger, hitting the ground directly in front of Henry. I pull back on the hammer as the beast lunges forward, diving toward me and Keagan.

"No!" Mr. Brent shouts, leaping into the way.

The two collide at my feet. The butler guards his face with his arms as Henry clamps his powerful jaws upon them, snapping the bones like twigs.

"Shoot him!" Keagan cries.

The remaining men flee farther into the maze.

"Hurry Devin!" Keagan yells as the black claws tear at Mr. Brent's clothes and head.

Henry lets out a fierce roar as he lifts his massive hand, ready to slash the old man's throat.

The beast's exposed chest is a welcomed target, and I pull the trigger. The ball breaks through the creature's thick fur and skin, causing him to recoil and cease from his attack upon Mr. Brent. Without thinking, I pull back on the hammer once again, turning the barrel and watching the final ball fall into place. I step closer, aiming at his heart and firing the gun. Henry turns away from the old man's body, yelping with intense pain. I haven't killed him, and I'm out of bullets. I can only hope I've mortally wounded him.

We all watch as Henry falls to the ground. He claws at his wounds as plumes of smoke rise from his skin. At first it's difficult to see, but as the clouds in the sky clear with the wind, the moon reveals the true damage of each wound. I cannot believe what is happening.

The surrounding flesh and bone are melting, dissolving, reacting to the bullet itself. I glance at the gun, wondering what the bullets are made of. If the myths about man beasts are true, they must be silver.

Keagan watches in horror as Henry writhes and wriggles in the open space. The beast's chest heaves quickly, and I notice something I didn't expect.

There's fear in Henry's eyes.

I've never wondered how intelligent such creatures could be. I suffer no regret as I watch Henry take his final breaths, but I wonder how much agency Henry had in his bloodlust. Perhaps he's the first and final victim of this curse. Henry grows still as death overtakes him.

"Come away," Mr. Brent says, his voice weak as he lay still on the ground. "You must get to the circle."

I go to the butler, inspecting his torn flesh and blood-soaked clothes. His injuries are worse than I thought, and his blood pools around him. "You need help."

I call out for the other servants to return, commanding Keagan to organize them.

"Nothing can be done," Mr. Brent says. "Go and tell Eliza the Stalker is dead. Swear your allegiance. You've proven your strength. . . but Alfred will kill . . . you if you do not swear it."

Mr. Brent takes in a painful breath as his voice fades, his whole body trembling with the exhale. "You belong . . . at Selene's side. You . . . you are . . . worthy of it."

Mr. Brent grows still.

I sit in shock. "Mr. Brent," I say, gently shaking him. "Jamison." I'm not sure I still have any emotion left in me as I rest my head upon his shoulders, hiding my falling tears. Slowly, the other men enter the space, each of them joining me in mourning the sudden loss of this unexpected hero.

He protected me. He risked his life.

"Look," Keagan says, his jaw dropped with shock.

I follow his gaze to Henry's dead body, moonlight now reflecting off smooth skin. Rising to my feet, I walk toward the carcass. It's no longer a beast lying in a heap upon the ground, but the naked form of a man. The human being rests on his side, deep wounds of melted flesh expose where the silver bullets struck the body. I inch my way closer, inhaling the smell of burnt flesh and sulfur.

As I step around the man resting dead at my feet and see his face, I expect to see a resemblance to the human portrait of Henry Addington displayed in the gallery.

To my complete shock, I stare instead at Mr. Jerome Rothbottom.

CHAPTER 24

Outside of the hedge maze, I sit with Keagan among the blades of grass as servants tightly wrap strips of fabric around my bare chest and ribs. A footman drapes my shirt back over me as they finish their work. It's stained with blood and sweat.

"It was Jerome all along," I whisper, still feeling numb from Mr. Brent's death. I wish I could mourn him properly, but I must make my way to the stone circle. And yet, something is nagging me.

"When we discovered the circle of stones during the party, Jerome was discussing Selene's engagement with Arthur. He never left the house."

Keagan glances around the open space surrounding us. His chest heaves as he freezes with concern. "You mean there's more than one of these creatures running around?"

I shrug at the thought but can't help my eyes from searching the grounds as well. "Jerome was engaged to Selene once before, so he's been through a Culling. Perhaps he was bitten." I feel ridiculous suggesting it, but it makes perfect sense.

"Having Henry pass on his curse?" Keagan wonders. "Assuming the creature we saw earlier was Henry Addington. Maybe it was one of Arthur's brothers-by-law or a crazy aunt. There could be generations of them."

More lightning fills the air as the clouds thicken, shrouding us in darkness.

Keagan places his hands upon his hips and bends his knees. We're both bruised and achy, but recovery is far from our minds.

"Why Jerome?" Keagan wonders.

"Perhaps it was his way of reconciling with the family, his penance for what he did to Selene. He tried to convince me he was a changed man, and I suppose he could have been speaking literally. But it's only a thought. I don't know what to believe. I certainly don't know who we saw earlier."

Keagan stares me down with a look of determination. "What if it's the price one pays to marry into the Addington family? If becoming a man beast is a requirement for keeping secrets, I will not take part in it. This isn't what I agreed upon when I signed the engagement contract."

The wind whips around us as lightning quickens in the distance.

I remain silent, contemplating the instructions Mr. Brent gave me. "We need to go to the circle of stones."

Keagan stops pacing and throws his hands up. "You're still going to follow through with this?"

He studies my eyes as I nod. "Arthur didn't give the final toast. Eliza is behind all this, and there must be a reason. I've killed the Stalker. The Culling is over. I need to tell her and—"

"And what?" Keagan asks. "Beg to be spared from turning into a vicious beast?"

His hands trembling, Keagan takes longer strides as he thinks out loud. "I have many homes on the mainland. We can hide there."

"We need to end this tradition," I say. "I thought killing Henry would do it, and perhaps that's still the answer. Whatever the answer is, we won't learn it until we go to the stones."

"I've heard of men trained to hunt the supernatural. We can call upon them. They can return here and destroy anyone else affected by this curse."

I balk at the suggestion. "Now you're the one who sounds bloodthirsty and insane."

He faces me, casting an acidic stare in my direction. "This is our chance to escape. Going to the circle of stones increases your probability of death. Can you honestly swear your allegiance to murderers?"

A part of me knows he's right. Selene did claim I would be insane to accept her family. But I can't turn away without answers.

I sigh, rubbing my sore ribs. "I'm not going to leave Selene. I love her. I told her nothing would change how I feel, and I am a man of my word. I trust Arthur won't allow me to be harmed. Mr. Brent said he's too weak against his brother, but I believe there is strength in numbers. Maybe with my objections along with Arthur's, we can stand against Alfred together. It'd be helpful if you were with me as well."

His face hardens. "You're honestly willing to risk your life all because of a woman and a foolish old man?" Lightning flashes, highlighting the disbelief upon his face. I nod, knowing how insane I appear to be.

"Unbelievable," he says. "You are more of a simpleton than I thought."

Thunder roars from the clouds, rattling my bones.

"I don't have the luxury of dropping everything on a whim and living as the upper-privileged do. Both Arthur and Selene have shown great kindness and charity. Perhaps it'll be enough to spare my life."

Keagan shivers. "If it's money you're worried about, I can help you."

"I will lose Selene if I go with you."

He steps closer. "And you will lose her when they kill you, whether by Henry's hand or by Alfred's. You know the truth now. You've seen what they are capable of."

I cast my gaze beyond Keagan, spying in the distance the main road leading back into town. I could join him, leave all this behind, leave Selene. But the thought of never seeing her again brings me to the brink of sadness. I don't want to leave her. Even Jamison said I was worthy. Earlier today she chastised me for not putting enough trust in her.

I'm choosing to put my trust in her now.

I stand, sighing deeply, and pat him on the shoulder. "I'm going to the circle of stones. I'm going to Selene."

Disappointed, Keagan turns away from me. "So be it. I'd wish you luck, but then I'd be the bigger fool. Goodbye, Mr. Foster. It has been a pleasure, all things considered."

I slick my hands through my hair and peer at the grove of willow trees. Taking one last glimpse at Keagan as he makes his way toward the main road, I begin my journey across the yard.

I walk toward my fate waiting for me at the far end of the lawn. Whether I am headed toward my salvation or my death, I do not know.

CHAPTER 25

Passing the topiary, I push through the willow trees, their tendrils snaking around me as if to swallow me whole. My lungs burn with each breath, and my side tenses whenever I try to run faster, but I move onward. My determination to see Selene gives life to my legs.

The storm has arrived. Lightning flashes with thunder crashing almost immediately afterward. Rain showers lightly over the teeming forest. The wind howls, swirling around me and breaking through the tall trees. Even nature opposes the misdeeds of this night.

Clearing the willows, I follow the path toward the circle of stones. The broken pillars glisten in the pale moon's light as I approach, but I see no sign of anyone else, human or beast.

I reach the closest stone pillar and press myself against it, resting my beating heart. The stone is cold and wet from the falling rain, bringing relief to my aching muscles and clammy skin. The thick forest surrounding this place weakens the wind until only a soft breeze reaches me.

I hope the end is near. I'm not sure how much more I can take.

I search the forest for movement, but my surroundings are void of any lurking creatures.

Still steadying my breath, I turn my gaze to the center of the circle. Rain collects in shallow puddles amongst the blades of grass. The moon's light breaks between patches of clear sky as the storm makes its way across the land.

I shiver, not from the cold rain but from the gross events of this location. I hesitate to cross into the grassy space.

This is a place of death.

A place where innocence was struck down due to someone's prejudice or disapproval. I still believe Arthur can stop this once and for all if I can only help him fight in some way.

Taking one last aching breath, I step into the circle of stones. My whole body tenses as I try to determine whether I'm still in danger or if my victory over Jerome has made me truly exempt from the cruel intentions of this horrible tradition.

I'm startled to see the Addington children behind the stone table, seemingly empty before I stepped within the circle. Each has their head bowed. Selene and Elara wear loose-fitted dresses tied at the waist and wrists. The fabric is thick as burlap but white as snow. Their hair cascades in waves past their shoulders, sticking to their skin in the falling rain, veiling their faces. From head to toe, Marcus and Quintin are dressed in red, their hands clasped in front of them. Each are silent, making no acknowledgement of my presence.

I want to call out to Selene, but I don't know if I should.

I stride toward them with all the courage I can muster, observing the stone altar now covered in an assortment of weaponry. Every hilt and handle are made of white ivory. The weapons are organized by size, the heavier and longer weapons are to the left, whittling down to smaller weapons on the right. Steel blades and gun barrels almost glow in the faded moon's light.

I recognize a slender blade among the swords and daggers. It's an isla sword, and according to one of Arthur's books, this sword, predating gunpowder, is particularly old and rare. I can't help but admire the jeweled guard and intricate etching at the base of the blade. From what I can tell, most of the weapons on display are possibly centuries old. Nobody uses a mace to defend themselves anymore.

I'm almost on the brink of rage that everyone who had faced the beast before tonight were able to defend themselves, but then I notice not one of the weapons are silver. I doubt my gun would have been loaded with silver bullets if it had been included in the collection for me to select from. Once the Guardian has designated prey, they're never intended to survive or even injure the beast in their struggle to live.

I stand across from Selene, the lightning flashing above us, highlighting her long, wet hair.

"The Stalker is dead," I say, my voice stern and confident, "I killed him using the weapon Mr. Brent provided for me." I pull the empty weapon from my pocket and place it on the altar. "Unfortunately, Mr. Brent didn't survive the attack. I don't know what to do, other than I swear my allegiance. I swear it with hopes you will understand . . ."

My words catch in my throat when Selene lifts her eyelids.

"Selene . . . you are—" The word refuses to escape my lips.

Moonbeams fall upon her face, accentuating the unnatural red glow gleaming through spindly strands of hair.

I gasp, "Is this possible? The moon is full and yet you are . . . you're human."

I step away from the altar, shuddering as all the Addington children now raise their heads, revealing their bright red eyes. Their stares are cold, their mouths frozen in a constant frown.

"I don't understand," I cry. "Why are you not beasts like Jerome?"

I take a moment to view each of them and wonder what they

will do to me.

"We are not slaves to the moon, Mr. Foster," Marcus says with a kind tone. "It is true," he continues to explain, "that we are the same creatures you recognize as man beasts. It is our family curse, passed down from Henry Addington. But instead of being the vicious beast you unfortunately witnessed this night, we have mastered the moment we shift between man and beast and back again. It is a secret we keep to protect our lives, for anyone who knows the truth holds our fate in their silence."

"Who did I see tonight during the party? Was it Henry?" I ask.

Marcus coughs a little, covering a laugh. "He's been dead for two hundred years."

Confused I glance at each of them. "Keagan and I saw a beast here just before the fireworks. Jerome was in the manor speaking with Mr. Addington."

Now it's the siblings' turn to exchange confused looks as they try to recall who might have been absent from the celebration at the time.

Reluctantly, Quintin speaks up. "There were so many reminders of Maggie and the night she died."

"You didn't attack us," I say, my heart pounding against my sore ribs.

A solemn look of determination washes over his face. "We Addingtons aren't mindless beasts."

Quintin proceeds to explain how after Henry's daughter Fiona married Pastor Black, her youngest sister and brother were to be married to their potential spouses. Henry upheld the first Culling to not repeat what happened with Mr. Netter. Both fiancés survived the evening but were still forced to accept Henry's bite so his secret was now theirs.

"He wasn't sure a human would be safe in his home, because months after his first transformation, he lost control and murdered his dearest wife beneath the full moon. After what he'd done to his sons and wife, Henry bit his surviving children and their spouses as well," Quintin says. "Giving them the power to protect themselves was the only way he could think of keeping them alive."

Marcus places a comforting hand upon his brother's shoulder.

My thoughts turn to Sophia and how she knew nothing about Quintin's family secret.

"Why didn't you tell your wife?" I ask him. "Such a commitment should require the utmost honesty."

Sighing, Quintin motions to his surroundings. "I never intended to return to this place. I can control the beast within, and I've never taken a life. In Delova there are miles and miles of trees. When the moon was full, and I needed to release the beast, I would leave Sophia with the impression I was stocking up on lumber for my carpentry. It wasn't entirely a lie, and with time, I wanted to tell her, but not like this."

Elara motions to the other Addington children. "My siblings and I, like all of Henry's direct descendants, were born with this curse. We do, however, wish to abolish this Culling tradition. Though we have no objections to showing our preternatural forms once we are betrothed or even threatening death to those with the knowledge to betray us, the Guardian should not be the one to determine who lives and who dies."

"Those born within the curse, carry it in their blood, waiting to be bitten." Quintin's voice becomes rough along with his cautious stare. He tells me how one could go a lifetime never knowing what they're capable of. But it is by the bite of another man beast which awakens the curse, awakens the beast within.

My head spins a little as I try to understand their explanations. "Arthur is the patriarch of this family. Why aren't his opinions considered?"

"Even for a moment, the beast must come out with the full moon," Marcus says. "If it is denied, with time both man and beast will weaken and eventually die."

Elara motions to their changed clothes. "We've already allowed our beasts to roam free tonight, but our father has resisted the change for some time. He's no match against his brother, the one designated to be the Guardian."

"Mr. Brent revealed to me Alfred's role as the Guardian," I say.

Marcus continues, his lips pursed in a tight frown. "What Elara has withheld is that our father has denied himself the shift ever since he took you on as an apprentice. He feels most human with you and sees you almost as a son. He never counted on you becoming a potential suitor, and by then he was powerless to protect you. With Jerome dead, we have a chance against Alfred . . ." He pauses, hesitating to say it.

"And our mother," Quintin says. His face softens as the rain steadily falls, puddling at his bare feet. "Do you know what has happened to Diane and Sophia? Have you seen them?"

Marcus remains stoic, clearly certain of Diane's safety, whereas Quintin fights a growing emotion as he waits for my answer. I respond with the deepest respect, acknowledging their escape from the library and intended destination. "I don't know what befell them after leaving the library, but if they made it to the cellar, I would assume they'll remain there until sunrise. I know now that Diane wasn't to be harmed, so I'm most concerned about Sophia."

Quintin's face contorts as he braces himself against the table. His chin quivers, and he wipes tears from his eyes. The torment he must be going through, wondering if Sophia is still alive. Suddenly, he pounds his fist on the table, but Marcus lovingly places a reassuring arm around his brother.

"And you, Marcus," I say. "Why couldn't you have left this place, like your brother? Why expose Diane to being bitten?"

Marcus glances toward the manor and chuckles, though he seems nervous. "You see how well leaving worked out for Quintin. But the truth is, Diane and I discussed that option, and in the end, she decided to participate in the Culling, should it be enforced in spite of my father's wishes. She wanted to remain in Anna's Cove society. I am one to respect the decisions of the woman I love, but I also feared for her. I didn't know if the Guardian would allow her to become an Addington, so I created the cellar where she'd be safe until the full moon passed and she could escape."

"And what of Keagan?" Elara says, her voice trembling in the cold rain. "He's not here, so obviously he must have perished."

I expect a look of grief, but instead the woman attentively waits for my answer with hope in her eyes. "Please tell me he's dead."

"Quite the opposite," I say. "He's fled." I neglect to say he spoke of seeking hunters. I wish I could deny any knowledge of his plans, but too many servants saw us go our separate ways.

At first Elara says nothing. She clasps her hands behind her back and lets out a deep sigh of disappointment.

"It is unfortunate to hear," she says, the red gleam in her eyes fading to a natural brown.

I step toward Selene, reaching for her. "Is this why you rejected me? Were you trying to protect me?"

She brushes the hair from her face and nods. "I couldn't stand the thought of you falling prey to all this. I wanted to tell you so many times, but that would only have put you at risk." A faint smile brushes across her face and she continues, "When my mother invited you to the celebration, my love blinded me into thinking she could possibly accept you as my father has—as I have," Selene says quietly, her soft lips quivering. "I should have known better. Please forgive me."

I'm not sure my heart could break any more than it already has, but to see the pained look on her face and hear her remorseful words nearly tears it to shreds. My beloved Selene is torn between the life she wishes to live and the life she's expected to uphold, and she was willing to sacrifice her own happiness to protect my life.

"I do forgive you." My words slip freely from my lips, prompting Selene to smile, if but for a moment.

"How touching." Eliza Addington's voice echoes from across the circle, accompanied by a flash of lightning. "Dearest Selene, you obviously shouldn't get too attached. He won't see the light of day. I guarantee it."

CHAPTER 26

In the shadow of the large oak trees, Eliza stands with Arthur and Alfred to either side. They're shrouded in black hooded cloaks. Arthur's and Alfred's smoldering red eyes fill the dark void around their faces. The three of them move together, walking closer to the circle of stones. Eliza is the first to remove her hood, revealing a different color in her eyes. They burn a fiery orange, as vibrant as crisp autumn leaves.

"Your eyes," I say, the words escaping my mouth without thought.

The woman turns her demonic gaze toward me, a smirk washing across her face. "A natural distinction of those brought into the curse."

I motion toward Addington Manor. "Jerome's eyes were red, like your children's." Even though he is a distant cousin, I assumed he'd been turned by a bite.

The older woman steps into the circle, keeping her attention directed toward me. She moves gracefully, her cloak soaking up water as she walks through puddles in the grass. "He comes from the family line of Henry's youngest son, Albert. You can add that to the many discoveries you've made about our family this evening." She raises gloved hands from beneath her wool cloak and clasps them at her waist. "It's sad to hear of Mr. Brent's passing. He was a good butler who I never thought would betray us. I can't help but wonder where he obtained such a weapon."

She gives an accusing look to Arthur. The man remains silent, keeping his attention to the ground.

"Never mind an insignificant servant," Eliza continues. "I'm more at a loss over Jerome. He would have made for a good addition to our family."

Jerome Rothbottom. I'm not ashamed to say how happy it makes me to know he's dead.

"How can you say such a thing?" Selene asks, speaking up from behind the altar. "He was cruel and unfeeling. Why did you allow him to come here when father already told him never to return?"

Eliza's eyes burn brighter as she speaks. "Because since he came into his inheritance, your union would have made you the most affluent family in all of Oxlin Providence. But now with him dead, that money will stay with the Rothbottoms." Eliza doesn't hide her annoyance at this turn of events.

Brushing her wet hair from her face, Selene cries out, "You were willing to match me with such an unruly man all because of status? Did you pay little attention to his disrespectful behavior when we were engaged?"

Eliza slowly makes her way toward her daughter, her steps precise and strong. "I was willing to overlook his imperfections. Sacrifices must be made to attain what status we hold. People in this society value those with greater riches, knowing opportunities of social gain come from associating with wealthier folks than they. And because of this, I have needed to work twice as hard to assure everyone the Addingtons are still worth respecting."

The Addington children exchange confused looks. Even I

perk an eyebrow.

"Still worth respecting?" Selene repeats. "Why would anyone suggest otherwise?"

"Ever since your father started extending his hobby to clients, there have been whispers of financial struggles. A wealthy man would never take on a vocation, unless he desperately needed to, so they assume we need the income. We were once guests in high demand with every family vying a match to one of our children, but invitations have waned in past months. Now we must rely on inviting others to our own gatherings, and we can't afford to be too exclusive with the invitations. Without the riffraff, we'd barely be able to fill a dining room table."

The engagement celebration tonight *was* filled with people who don't receive invitations to the most elite parties, but I'd hardly call them riffraff. They were mostly of high status with their wealth coming from the production of goods, such as Harold's winery.

But could this social stigma really be enough to murder innocent people?

I step toward the older woman, focusing on exactly what she means. "Rumors? All of this is happening because people are gossiping about the Addington wealth?" I can't contain myself. "You killed so many people tonight just because you fear what others might think about your financial status?"

Eliza shrugs. "I told Jerome he could do as he pleased with those who were still inside, as long as he didn't harm Diane or Keagan. Mr. Brent did try to get the servants to safety, so Jerome only harmed those who disobeyed. Not a desirable quality in a servant."

"Wretched woman, have you no regard for human life?" I ask, my pale eyes burning into hers.

"Do you know how insulting it is to have the help sleeping on the same level as the family?" she asks with a whine. "Servants belong beneath the main level, out of sight and out of mind. But my foolish husband moved the servants up to the second floor and also gave each of them raises, both in spite of my protests. Between the renovations and the salaries, he's depleted our finances by a third. Add the constant social gatherings I must host to keep the Addington name prominent, and I might as well assume we're on the brink of financial ruin.

"I needed to take matters into my own hands. If my husband wanted to bring the servants into our living quarters, then I would bring the Culling into our living quarters as well. At least with the depletion of employees, there will be more money to invest in upcoming social gatherings."

My jaw hurts from clenching it so tightly. I must look away from her in order to calm the anger growing within me. I suppose I should be more afraid at the sight of her unnatural orange eyes, but something within me only sees the woman as a petty creature undeserving of such a reaction.

"So you uphold the vilest tradition?" I ask. My chest tightens with anger.

Such pettiness. Such unnecessary pettiness.

Eliza nods, her eyes looking me over from head to toe. "I'm more concerned with saving my family than upholding any tradition. The tradition just happened to be the best way to save my family. Had Jerome fulfilled his agreement with the Guardian and killed you and Sophia, Arthur would have been forced to reconcile to Jerome's marriage to Selene or fight him to the death. Since my husband bears not an ounce of courage or wolven strength, Selene would have married Jerome and become the wealthiest woman in this horrid little town, restoring the Addington name. Everyone could stop their speculations."

"So it's true!" Quintin shouts, stepping out from behind the table. Again Marcus holds him back. "You promised Sophia wouldn't be harmed! I knew you were lying."

"Now is not the time to fight," Marcus says. He has Quintin in a tight embrace.

Quintin submits to his brother. "She's just like grandfather. I'm a fool for believing her."

Laughing at her son, Eliza places her hands upon her hips. "I will not throw away all I've established as a successful wife and mother because my selfish children think it is important to follow their hearts. At least Marcus and Elara understand the importance of duty over emotion."

I glance at the mentioned children. Marcus places a comforting arm around Elara as she lowers her head in shame.

"This must stop at once," Quintin shouts. "Please, Father, do something. As patriarch of the family, you must be able to do something."

"It is Eliza who enforces the Culling," Alfred says, stepping into the circle of stones. "It begins and ends at her command. If she orders the prey must be killed, then it is so."

"You see how this has affected our family," Quintin says, pointing at Alfred's hands. "I see no ring upon your finger, but as a man of wealth and means you could have easily found a spouse. Even you, the Guardian, will not subject anyone to this horrible tradition."

A deep guttural growl comes from Alfred. "Do not speak of things you know nothing about."

Quintin walks closer, standing beside his father. "I know why you couldn't defend my Maggie. You were engrossed with this tradition, with how this family has upheld wealth over all other qualities in a potential spouse. You've fought against your upbringing as of late. Are you willing to fight a little more?"

Finally, Alfred removes his hood. He grinds his teeth as he hides his body within the large cloak. "Enough of this foolishness. The Culling is about far more than wealth. We share the curse to protect the secret that has the power to destroy us."

"If that were true, then the Guardian would not select suitors for prey based on their fortunes. We can't deny the fact that only the wealthiest survive." Arthur lowers his hood.

"It's the only way to ensure our survival," Alfred argues.

"There is another way," Arthur says. He stands tall beside his son. "This tradition can end with us. Whoever would love my children should be given the choice to accept the curse or not, depending upon their own agency and their trust in my children's self-mastery over the beast within. The curse would continue within our bloodline, passing from generation to generation, dormant. So what if there are wretched whispers about what we are? People are less inclined to believe such stories these days. If we openly speak of what Henry did and say the rumor started with him, we can control the narrative."

Alfred sneers at his brother, following with a sharp point of his finger. "We control the narrative now, and it's kept us safe! We all know that the assurance of our destruction is the best way to create an unbreakable contract, which is why each Addington must accept the curse. Who would accept it if given a choice?"

"I would," I say, drawing everyone's attention to me.

My heart races as I focus on each pair of eyes staring at me. "Just because I've discovered what you are doesn't change *who* you really are, does it? I swear my allegiance not only because I love Selene and would wish to marry her someday, but I swear it because there is no greater man I would rather associate myself with than Arthur Addington." I face Arthur, determined to assure him of my loyalty. "You have shown the utmost kindness and respect to all. I'm forever indebted to you."

"Of course you would want to associate with my brother," Alfred growls. "You're poor and insignificant. By marrying Selene, you'd have access to more wealth than you could ever imagine."

It's true. I won't deny it. But I continue my declaration of loyalty and say, "I am not a charlatan. I love Selene not as a trinket to display but as a companion, and I would feel the same no matter her status in society. I have found an honorable example of the kind of man I should be, not only because of Selene but because of Mr. Addington as well."

Arthur walks to his wife and takes her by the arm. "Please, Eliza," he says, "you must stop worrying what others may think about our family. With all of the wild animal attacks or hunting accidents that have befallen fiancés, it's a miracle anyone thinks highly enough of us to want to marry an Addington. The world is changing, and our children will love who they love or they will leave. Quintin and Selene may be headstrong, but they are showing us what the future of this family looks like. The tradition that's meant to hold us together is tearing us apart. We've already murdered Quintin's fiancée, and now that he's found love again, we may have killed his wife. He will never forgive us, and we shouldn't ask him to."

Arthur looks at Quintin. "You may to go and find your wife. I hope she's well. And if I never see you again, you have my blessing, my love and the knowledge that I will do everything in my power to end this."

"No, Father," he says. "I will see this to the end, trusting she is safe with Diane. I choose to remain here, with you."

A loud huff escapes Eliza. "And what of Keagan Bottrell?" she asks, her eyes burning like hot embers. "What are you going to do about him?"

Elara leans forward, catching her mother's attention. "I will tend to him, Mother," she says.

Eliza only shakes her head. "You couldn't tend to him before the Culling. No. Once I have put an end to Mr. Foster, I will tend to Mr. Bottrell myself."

Fear overcomes me as Selene and I lock eyes. So this is still to be my fate?

"The Stalker is dead! The Culling is over!" Arthur shouts, his eyes blazing with emotion.

"It isn't over until I say it's over!" Eliza shouts back. "You have no right to make demands, Arthur. Such rights were forfeit the moment you turned your back on your obligations as an Addington. Now, move aside, or you will suffer with him. Mr. Foster must die!"

CHAPTER 27

Eliza proceeds to remove her cloak and gloves, but Arthur grabs her shoulders, staring into her eyes.

"Please, Eliza, end this now. No more innocent blood must be spilt."

Shaking her head, Eliza pulls free of his grasp, tossing her gloves to the soaked ground. "You are not the man I married, and it pains me to see you in such a weak state of mind. When my life was spared the night of our engagement celebration, I vowed to uphold the family name. I suffered so much and all for the Addingtons—all for you."

"I love you," Arthur says. "If you love me, you'll stand by me. You must see what it's doing to our family."

"You've betrayed me. There is no love between us anymore. There hasn't been for years."

Arthur winces at her declaration but perseveres. "Then end this for Selene if you won't end it for me. Devin killed Jerome, and according to the rules, he should be spared."

191

"That was hardly a fair fight," Eliza says, shaking her head at Arthur.

"And this is?" Arthur goes to the altar and begins pushing the weapons to the ground. "Not one of these can harm us!" None of the children flinch as their father sends blades and guns hurling across the altar. Apart from some torn fabric, the weapons do no harm.

The rain has finally stopped, but the clouds still brush across the sky, dimming the moon's light. Arthur begs one last time for Eliza to reconsider what she's doing, but his pleas fall upon deaf ears.

"This has gone on too long," she says, her voice deepening.

Eliza transforms. Thick brown fur grows instantly all over her body. Falling to the ground, she pulls herself into a tight ball. The sound of cracking bones and tearing flesh makes me shudder. Her bright orange eyes fix upon Arthur. Staring with shock, I watch her jaw crack and unhinge. Eliza lets out another yell as her face elongates, her nose and upper lip fusing together as they protrude, covering a row of sharp teeth and long fangs. A long, bristled tail sweeps across the grass. Her clothes and skin tear free of her now larger frame, and her skin dissolves into a pulpy mesh at her feet. She stands slowly, her chest heaving with deep breaths, and lets out a deafening roar.

"Devin," Selene cries, "you must defend yourself at once." From the ground, she picks up the isla sword, offering it to me. Immediately, she grimaces as her hand makes contact with the blade. A silver blade.

"Take it! It will keep you safe," she says, her stoic face keeping her deadly secret.

Elara tears a bit of her own dress to wrap around Selene's hand, flashing a stern look between me and her newly transformed mother.

Eliza falls upon all fours and charges. Her orange eyes blaze against the brown tufts of fur on her hideous face. She lunges for me, and I dodge, sending her crashing into the altar. Selene's siblings scramble out of the way.

Eliza recovers quickly. She's much smaller than Jerome, her sleek and able body standing as tall as an average man. I try to run, but she's too fast. Grabbing my shoulders, she forces me into the puddling water surrounding us. Mud and rain mix in my eyes and splash into my mouth. I twist from her grasp as she raises her hands, preparing to bash in my chest. Avoiding the attack, I painfully turn away from her heavy hands. Water sprays from the impact of fists against the ground.

Standing, I swipe at her with the blade, forcing her to give me space. We circle one another. Eliza's ears are turned back, and her eyes never leave my face. She's unconcerned about my weapon, believing it harmless to her.

Clasping the hilt with both hands, I slash at her massive shoulder, only to miss when she bats me away. Her sharp claws slice into my forearm with brute force.

I try again to keep Eliza at a distance, catching her arm with the blunt side of my blade. She recoils as the silver singes her fur and blisters her skin.

The impact also affects my sword, the metal dissolving from the contact like paper reacting to the heat of a small flame. The tip of the blade falls to my feet, but I'm bolstered with courage in seeing how easily she's wounded.

Eliza claws at me, scraping the blade. The sound of her claws against the metal pierces straight to my inner ear. I react as she slashes my arm, my blood mixing with the damp fabric, creating a morbid watercolor of red. I dodge another advance, seeing from the corner of my eye Arthur racing toward me.

"Eliza! Stop!" Arthur shouts. "You'll die!"

He tries to come between Eliza and me, but Alfred takes him by the collar and pins him against the nearest pillar.

"Do not interfere, dear brother, or you'll suffer the consequences," Alfred says as his fingertips press against Arthur's throat.

"I must stop them!" Arthur says between gasps.

"Then you will die!" Alfred roars. His face starts to change, and he releases Arthur as his body transforms.

"Run to the forest!" Arthur shouts, racing toward Eliza and pushing her away. She stumbles and lands on her haunches. "I will hold her back so you don't have to fight."

He's pulled away by Alfred, who has now fully transformed into a vicious beast.

"Father!" Quintin yells.

He runs toward Alfred, his red eyes blazing, removing his clothes as he transforms almost instantly. Marcus joins in the fight, ignoring Elara's pleas to stop. As soon as he clears the altar, he too transforms.

The two brothers leap upon Alfred, separating him from Arthur, their bodies twisting in order to weigh the man beast down. I can't tell the difference between the brothers and Alfred, for all three are practically identical in size and color. One beast is tossed to the ground as another slashes its chest.

With no one in her way, Eliza stands on all fours and charges toward me. Arthur reaches for her but is left with a handful of fur.

I dodge Eliza's advances, finding myself trapped between a pillar and her long claws.

"Hide in the forest," Arthur says. "When the sun rises, the beast will weaken, and everyone will be human again. I'll try to hold her off until then."

She swipes, and I duck as her long claws leave deep marks in the stone.

I glance at the sky, recognizing the hint of dawn upon the horizon. The storm clouds are fading as the moon dips toward the distant hills.

"But what if you can't?" I ask, my attention on Eliza as she prepares to spring.

"Don't worry about me." Arthur's dark eyes light up like torches as he charges toward Eliza. He doesn't shift but maintains his human form as he grabs her wrist and pulls her away from me. I take one last look at my dearest Selene and, with sword in hand, I run into the forest.

CHAPTER 28

Racing through the forest, I grasp my side tightly in an attempt to lessen the stings caused by the constant need to balance myself. I don't dare look over my shoulder. I'm afraid of what I'll see.

Coming to a fallen tree, I climb atop it, my muscles aching with each push and pull. Leaping from it into a small stream, I follow it for a ways, making my trail harder to follow. I come to rainwater flowing into the stream over a low incline and climb through the water to hide my footprints. Every time the breeze brushes against my body, I shiver. Every moment becomes a challenge as I tremble not only from the cold but from the pain my body has endured this night.

I don't know how much farther I can go. There's no place to hide, no thicket to seek shelter in. There are only trees, shrubs, and creeping foliage.

I can hear the echoes of beasts roaring behind me.

I duck behind a large tree, resting myself against the trunk.

I'm not sure how much longer I have until the sun rises. My mind races over everything I've witnessed. The transformation from man to beast is unbelievable. The beast itself is terrifying. I think of the servants in Addington Manor and Mr. Brent in the hedge maze, all dead because of the bloodlust brought on by rage and enhanced by a wretched curse. I trust Arthur means it when he says others will have the choice to become like the family. I love Selene and still wish to be by her side, but after seeing the transformation with my own eyes, I'm no longer so certain that I can accept the same curse pulsing through my veins.

On the other side of the trees, I hear footsteps coming closer. Eliza must have found me. I'm far away enough from the circle of stones. Far away enough from Selene. If I'm to meet my end, at least my beloved will be spared my final cries. Eliza draws closer as I force myself to backtrack away from the trees. I can hear her moving through the bushes, her swift steps matching my racing heart.

Though I possess no strength compared to these creatures, I'm tired of running. I come to a clearing and dig my heels into to the soft ground. I face Eliza's direction and I hold tightly to my weapon.

The steps are drawing closer now. I see something stir in the foliage.

If I am to die, Eliza better make it quick.

"Devin?" Selene's voice calls from the bushes.

My beloved steps from the natural barrier and smiles. She greets me with a hug. My muscles tense from the embrace, prompting a nervous apology from Selene.

"What are you doing here? You shouldn't interfere," I say. "Though I suspect you've already done so." I hold up the isla sword.

Selene looks at her bandaged hand. "Quintin tried to convince me to leave with him after what happened to Maggie. I refused, but he begged me to consider that none of my suitors would have a chance, as I don't measure a man's value by his fortune. His words remained with me all these years. But it was Marcus who inspired me to anticipate the worst. As soon as Marcus announced his official engagement to Diane, I had a few of the weapons gilded in silver. Regardless of your participation in Culling, I couldn't allow Marcus to face the same possible fate as Quintin.

"In preparation for the Culling, servants are selected to place the weapons upon the altar. My father wasn't harmed when he brushed the weapons to the ground because he made no direct contact with the blades against his skin."

I gently touch her hair and stare into her beautiful brown eyes. "I'm sure it was difficult for you to do, knowing your deadly reaction to silver, and that it would be used to kill someone in your family," I say. "I'm grateful that it's kept me safe. With dawn coming, I hope to prevent using lethal force. It's hardly appropriate to ask for a woman's hand after killing her mother."

Selene smiles sadly at the absurdity of this truth, but quickly returns to the urgency of the moment.

"My father tried to stop my mother but she's too strong for him. She had a moment to strike him down, but instead she caught your scent on the breeze. She's still pursuing you. I ducked away the moment Quintin and Marcus subdued Alfred. Elara is returning to the manor to help where she can."

Selene wraps her arms around me again, ignoring the filth I'm covered in. "I'm so sorry I've made you a part of this, but if you survive until sunrise, you'll prevail. Not far from here is Henry's old cellar. Barricade yourself in there while I distract my mother."

"She already has my scent. I'll be trapped in the cellar."

Selene looks at my soiled shirt. Her cheeks turn a few shades of pink. "We simply need to bide our time. Give me your shirt. I can use it to draw off your scent and give you more time to hide."

My cheeks flush a little. I've never engaged in such an intimate act as removing my shirt in the presence of a fair lady.

"I—I suppose it could . . . help."

I lift the heavy cotton free of my belt and try to hoist it over my shoulders but wince and let go.

"Let me help you," Selene says, carefully touching the fabric with her fingertips.

I anticipate Eliza is just around the corner. A growing fear boils within the pit of my stomach. I should be running, fleeing from Eliza, but I worry more for Selene, fearing the consequences of her interference.

Gently, Selene slips the garment over my head, taking a moment to linger with her gaze. By the glint in her eyes, she's not too put off by the sight of me.

"You should get to the cellar. I'll try to lead her in the opposite direction."

"Will I see you again?" I ask, not wanting to leave.

Selene looks over her shoulder. Eliza can't be too far away. I frantically glance beyond her and see nothing, but I hear the rustle of bushes in the distance. I don't know what will happen next, and if I am to die, I refuse to die with regrets. Wrapping an arm around Selene, I press my lips firmly against hers. In return Selene grabs my shoulders and holds me close to her. We continue to kiss, though I know I must leave. I feel her heart beating against my chest as the lingering desire to stay in her presence threatens to overwhelm me.

I move my lips to her cheek, attempting to pull away. She releases her tight embrace and rests her head upon my bare chest.

"Head north until you find the rotted cellar doors," she says. "Go now."

Eliza clears the foliage in front of us. She spreads her arms, her fur now matted and wild.

"Mother, you've lost," Selene says. "He will kill you if you continue. No one wants you to go to your death. Forfeit this fight."

Eliza growls and crouches, preparing to strike her daughter. I start to flee, but I can't help looking over my shoulder. Selene is endangering herself for me, and I don't feel it's right that I leave her now.

Selene drops my shirt as claws grow from her nailbeds. Fully transformed into her beastly figure, Selene stands as tall as her mother but with thick black fur. An inhuman sound escapes her, warning Eliza to stay away.

Eliza doesn't yield. She grabs Selene, slamming her against a tree. Stunned by the motion, Selene recovers and digs her claws deep into Eliza's stomach, forcing the creature to recoil. Selene shuffles after her mother, knocking her to the ground. Clawing and biting ensues. Both creatures pummel and tear at each other's flesh.

I can't look away. I grip the sword, keeping a close eye on the fight and ready to end it if necessary to save Selene.

I think Selene gains the advantage over her mother, lashing at her constantly, but Eliza blocks the onslaught of blows and slaps Selene with so much force it knocks her unconscious.

"Selene!" I stare at the lifeless body.

I extend my blade, and rush to defend her helpless form, my whole body trembling. I stare into Eliza's orange eyes.

We circle one another until Eliza advances. I, too, advance, swinging my sword as she bats it away, her claws slicing the flesh of my side. I try again, hacking the air, missing her by inches. Another stinging jab of her claws dig into my wounded side, her plump fingers forcing their way through my muscle, her claws breaking through my ribs.

I cry out as our eyes meet. Her sour breath fills my nostrils.

I stare at the sharp fangs and lift my blade, swinging it sideways. My aim is intended for her throat, but the remains of my silver blade lodge deep into the thick flesh of her right shoulder.

An ear-piercing scream breaks from Eliza, and she tosses me aside like a rag doll. I make impact with the hard ground, my hot blood mixing with my soiled bandages. Eliza cries out as she grasps the sword, still stuck in its fleshy sheath. Slowly and painfully, she removes the hilt, the blade all but disintegrated into her body now. Drops of silver and blood fall in thick globs down her arm and to her feet. Tossing aside what remains of my weapon, she digs at her wound, clearing it as she's done before. I watch the silver spread like fire, turning her muscle into mush. Her arm will likely fall off if she's unsuccessful in removing the silver.

With Eliza distracted, I get to my feet. Selene remains motionless, still in her beastly form. I pray she's not dead. I turn away from Eliza and try to run, but my vision blurs as I lean against a nearby tree. It's difficult to breathe. I'm unarmed, wounded, and exhausted, but I only need to survive until daybreak. How much longer?

I push forward, hoping I'm headed in the right direction of the cellar. Blazing a trail, I find myself on an incline. My fingers grab the soft dirt in front as I stagger through the foliage.

I don't know what to do. Another roar echoes, much quieter now, behind me. I keep running, step after heavy step.

I trip over a large stone and fall flat onto a wooden cellar door. The wood is rotted, giving easily beneath my weight.

I tumble into the hole, landing hard on my side six or seven feet below. The loud rattle of dried wood scraping against stone bounces off the mold-covered walls. The area is small, perhaps five feet in width, and the air smells of mildew and rot. I try not to cry out as I lift myself to a sit.

Morning is dawning, and my eyes adjust to what little light floods into the area. The space extends beyond the faded stream of light from the hole above me. I feel around the floor for anything I can use as a weapon and my hand finds a branch. I lift it, and the smooth edges slide in my palm. This isn't a branch. I hold it up in the increasing light. At first it looks like a dried out sponge, but upon closer examination it dawns on me what particular object I'm holding.

It's a broken bone.

Dropping it, I shudder, not knowing whether it belongs to a

human or an animal.

More bones are at my feet. Kicking away the litter of morbid debris, I press my aching back against the cold wall.

Thick chains clang beside me. I grasp one, feeling a curved piece of metal at its end.

"Shackles," I breathe. "They're shackles."

I look around the room, seeing piles of bones collecting in the corners. This cellar was built in order to keep Henry's family safe whenever he transformed. I look at the stone walls, tracing the scratch marks.

Beside my foot is a pile of clothes filled with discolored holes. Human victims.

This was the final resting place of those who didn't survive the Culling. Quintin's Maggie lies here, and if Sophia didn't make it to Marcus's secret cellar, she'll be tossed here as well.

My muscles tense, stopping me from moving any farther. I'm frozen with fear and trapped. If Eliza finds me, I might as well be waiting in my grave.

A rusted ladder leads up to the hole I fell through. The dim light of dawn permeates through the storm, revealing more about the cellar. I can see more piles of bones in the corners and overgrown tree roots breaking through the weak mortar in between stone bricks.

I take a deep breath and limp toward the ladder. Grasping the rusty rung, I try making the ascent. I get halfway before a familiar sound fills me with dread.

Above me, Eliza stares with eyes bright as glowing embers. A deep guttural growl breaks from her throat, and she bares her teeth.

I'm done for. There's no way to escape, and I'm not fit to fight. As least Selene isn't around to witness my end. I pray she's all right.

Carefully, I step down from the ladder, keeping a close watch on Eliza as she crouches near the ground.

I reach for the nearest bone fragment, its jagged edge

reminding me of a dagger.

Eliza's whole body stiffens, and she leaps into the cellar, landing directly on me. I struggle, stabbing the bone against her thick fur, but it does nothing. We roll to the side as Eliza attempts to bite at my neck and shoulders.

I hold her back.

We grapple with one another over the bones. Jagged pieces of debris dig into my back as she pins me down. I yell, shielding my face as her massive jaws clamp down on my arm. I hear a loud crack as the bone breaks in two. I can't unlock her strong bite.

My blood seeps from the wound, dripping onto my loose bandages.

Eventually, Eliza unhinges her jaws, her fangs unsheathing from my flesh. My arm falls against my chest. I have no power left in me to fight or move. She towers over me, her body blocking my view of the brightening sky. Why isn't she weakening?

Eliza gives one final roar before biting onto my shoulder, missing my throat entirely. She wants me to suffer, not die quickly.

My bones crunch, filling me with complete and utter pain. Eliza jostles me like a dog capturing a small creature. Her teeth tear free of my flesh. My blood covers her large mouth. She bites again, this time near the crook of my neck. What little energy within me spills upon the ground along with my blood. My limbs grow heavy, and everything slowly fades into darkness.

BANG!

Eliza whimpers and tears away from me.

BANG!

She arches her back as if struck, her excruciating cries bounce off the stone walls, piercing my inner ear like nails upon shale.

Her hot blood spills over my face and onto my skin and mingles with my own.

I cast my eyes to the hole, wanting to see the face of my

savior. None of the Addingtons would kill Eliza. It must be a servant. But why would a servant risk the family's wrath for me? My blurring vision focuses on the morning sun's light finally beaming through the forest.

Arthur Addington holds a gun in both hands. His face is cold. His eyes are now their regular, dark brown color.

I try to speak, but nothing comes. No sound escapes me.

Eliza's monstrous body begins to return to her human form as she takes her final breaths on top of me.

Selene lingers in my thoughts as everything goes black.

CHAPTER 29

It's daytime. Light fills my vision as I rest upon a comfortable bed in a large room. My body is clean, and I wear a fresh pair of clothes. Touching my neck and shoulder and arm, I realize my wounds are gone. What remains are rough purple scars from Eliza's bite, drawing a terrifying image of her rage and bloodlust. I take in a deep breath, expanding my lungs, feeling no pain from my ribs. My arm is healed, and I feel better than ever.

In all the times I've imagined what the Creator's Hall looked like, I never pictured a convalescence room. But perhaps my soul must heal from the mortal physical wounds that sent me here.

The faint sound of a happy tune fills the air. I push myself to a sit and look around. I'm alone in the well-lit room. The tune resonates in my mind as I carefully get out of bed.

"Hello?" I call, hoping to discover who is humming the pleasant melody. Perhaps they know how one navigates the afterlife.

When I get no response, I walk to the doorway and peek into the hall.

I'm in the servant quarters of Addington Manor. I recognize the long floor rug and potted plants. The hall is spotless and clean. Am I now to haunt this manor? Watching Selene court and marry another would kill me again.

There's not a soul around, living or dead.

"Selene? Arthur?"

The humming grows louder as I make my way to the door leading to the library. It's a lullaby, a simple song my mother hummed before putting me to bed. She must be here to greet me.

I enter the library, warmth filling me as I anticipate a reunion. The woman humming sits in an armchair across the room. I can't see her face, but I see her hand upon the armrest, tapping to the slow beat.

"Mother?" I call.

The humming stops, and everything is silent.

"Devin, my dear, are you here?" the woman replies.

I walk closer, the floorboards creaking beneath my weight. "Mother?" I ask again, nearing the chair.

I take the woman's hand and kneel, but as I look to the woman's face, I draw away. The wretched woman who sits within the armchair and hums the beautiful tune is none other than Eliza Addington.

Her eyes glow like orange embers, and a low growl draws from her throat. I step away as she shifts into her beastly form, her claws scraping against the hardwood floor.

What great sin have I committed to deserve this for eternity? "No," I cry. "This can't be happening."

I try to flee, but she trips me. I call for Selene as Eliza digs her claws deep into my flesh. I can't get away. I can't fight.

Eliza forces me onto my back and releases a deafening roar. I watch in terror as her sharp claws dig into my chest, breaking through my ribs and tearing out my heart. Death does not come to offer relief.

"No!" I shout, sitting up in bed, tossing the blankets off my body. "Let me die!" I scream at the top of my lungs. My chest heaves as I examine my body once again, seeing all is well and intact. "She . . . she's killing me." I steady my breath and rest my back on the pillow.

The room which I've woken in is much different than the one before. I rest within a canopy bed, mauve curtains tied to each post. Large windows across the room warm a long upholstered bench for sitting. Beside the bed is a large dresser and wardrobe made of black mahogany, matching the bed frame and other pieces of furniture.

Everything is warm and comfortable. I listen warily for my mother's lullaby. What terrors await me now?

"Mr. Foster!" Hattie cries, pushing the door open. "You're awake! Oh, thank the Creator and all that is good in this world!"

I flinch away, expecting her to draw a knife or even transform, but she sets the fresh linens she's carrying on the bench and clasps her hands with joy. "You've had such terrible dreams, but we were unable to wake you. I'm so glad you're back with us."

A terrible dream? Could it be? Or is this a false hope intended to create more torment when it's torn away?

I search for clues, my eyes catching a large painting of Elara above the dresser. She sits in a comfortable chair, her hands placed in her lap and her shoulders turned slightly. The background is plain with faded brown and beige strokes blending to highlight her baby blue dress. It's odd seeing her in a light color, and I wonder why she doesn't wear them more often, as this lovely blue accentuates her eyes.

From where I sit upon the bed, which I take to be Elara's, I notice a slight glint of red painted among the dark brown strokes of her irises. This must be another dream. I shouldn't be able to see such detail from this distance. And would the family hide their secret in plain sight, even if nobody besides family members and the most trusted servant would be allowed in Elara's bedroom to see this portrait's nod to the beast within?

Perhaps Elara will attack next. I watch the door.

Bowing, Hattie pulls the door open wider. I brace myself for the attack, but no person or beast enters.

"I shall inform Mr. Addington of your progress," she says. "My deepest expression of gratitude for keeping us safe. I'm grateful you survived."

She pauses and gives me a warm smile before scuttling into the hallway.

I relax a little and look over what remains of my wounds, finding no proof of injury. I step out of the bed, feeling the warm rug with my toes. I take in a deep breath, detecting a hint of lavender where Hattie walked across the room. I can smell it so precisely I could trace her path.

Eliza bit me. Am I one of them now? Am I alive? I pinch my arm and feel the pain, then shake my head. That only tells me I'm not dreaming. I could still be dead. How exactly does one determine whether they're alive?

"Devin, it is good to see you awake," Arthur says from the doorway, startling me. His face looks happy, but his posture speaks of grief and exhaustion. This must be Arthur in the flesh.

I sigh. What does one say to the man who saved your life by killing someone he loved?

"I am," I say, my voice barely breaking from my lips. My throat is dry.

Arthur motions for me to return to the bed as he requests a footman bring him a chair. He stands sullenly, keeping quiet. He's dressed in black, a suit of mourning. He wears a black ring on his finger to signify the death of his wife.

I sit on top of the bedcovers and watch the footman leave, closing the door behind him. There's a glass of water on the bedside table, and I take a drink.

"How are you feeling? Are you well?" Arthur asks.

I nod, still speechless. He could have allowed me to die. He didn't need to protect me. I can't imagine killing Selene, even if it were to save an innocent life.

"I'm sorry for your loss," I say.

Politely, Arthur bows his head, acknowledging my sentiment. "The funeral was a few days ago. You've been asleep for over a week. That's natural, though. Your body is recuperating from the attack and adjusting to the internal infection which comes with it. I don't think we should think upon it as a curse any longer, however."

So it's true. I am alive, and I believe I owe my life to the Addington . . . infection. My stomach churns at the thought of my future. I fear the pain of transforming, the shifting of my bones and tearing of my muscles. But the one thought which lingers, which gives me pause, is what kind of monster will I become beneath the full moon.

Arthur awkwardly clears his throat and taps his foot nervously on the floor. "I'm not good at explaining these sorts of things. Eliza was meant to help our new members through the change. I should tell you that Diane has accepted Marcus's bite and is resting in Selene's room."

"And what is expected of me?" I ask.

Arthur sits straight in his chair and runs his hands along his legs, resting them upon his knees. "Devin, please understand, you will survive this. It's not fatal. No matter how much pain you experience in the weeks to come, it will pass."

The grave look upon his face frightens me. "Go on."

"You will drift in and out of a horrible state of mind. You won't know what is real or what is false. You'll sleep but experience night visions and wake still trapped within them. You'll swing between a barrage of emotions. It's all a reaction to Eliza's saliva flooding your system. Every cell in your body will change to become capable of allowing you to shift between man and beast."

Such talk from Arthur is expected, using more scientific terms than archaic. To call the family curse an infection eases my nerves, despite the impending fate of transformation.

I imagine the mental torment one must face when feeding upon live animals, or worse—human flesh. I pray I never take a life of innocence.

Arthur leans closer, resting his arms upon the bed as he stares into my eyes. "In order to prepare your body for your first transformation, your muscles will constrict and release unexpectedly, gradually building up the support of your increased strength and speed. This will begin in a few days, bringing no relief until it's time to shift."

He continues, his concentration enhanced by focusing on my condition. "You will reject food and water, but the infection will keep you alive and strong. You'll feel a hunger and thirst that nothing will satiate until the moon's pull upon your frame releases the monster within.

"But I only call it a monster at first, because nothing will stop it from wanting to feed. When the time comes, we'll remove you from Addington Manor and place you within Henry's cellar. You will feed upon the flesh of an animal, which we will provide. You mustn't fight your transformation. You must allow the pain to overtake you. Each time your muscles constrict, every time the vilest things enter your mind, every scathing emotion which takes over—you must accept it. The darkness must be embraced before it will be overcome."

I lift a hand to stop him, snapping him out of his deep expository trance. "Marcus said that if one doesn't transform, then both man and beast will weaken and die. He also said you hadn't transformed for months. Why?"

Sighing, Arthur lifts his gaze to the heavens. "Yes, it's true. Ever since I took you on as an apprentice, I've denied the beast within. I experienced a change when I embraced the responsibility as a teacher. I won't deny how coming to see you as a son and imagining myself as human, completely human, gave me a moment to feel as other fathers do. The life of an Addington is so different compared to other families. But now, finding you in the physical state you are in reminds me how I will never truly escape who I am."

Pressing his back against his chair, he sighs again, his hands clapping against his knees. "I wish you didn't have to go through this transformation. I wish you could have discovered our family secret under different circumstances. I encouraged my children to not be afraid of what they are, as much as I contradicted such encouragement. I specifically demanded Marcus tell Diane of our family curse and of the Culling tradition, and I promised him it would never happen again. Eliza may have forced the Culling, but I intend it to be the absolute last."

I can't help but notice the sad look in his eyes. "I'm sorry about your wife. I know how much you loved her."

My words induce a shrug from the man.

He slouches as he casts his attention to the floor. "At her funeral, our guests remarked on how outspoken she was. I always admired her confidence and talents.

"She upheld the social expectations and was good at it, but the focus of greed and power passed from one Addington generation to the next warped her sense of responsibility. So much obligation is placed upon a woman—tending to the family, servants, and husbands while also adhering to each and every ridiculous social rule.

"I tried to encourage her to seek interests beyond the typical. She loved decorating the home, finding beauty where none-else could." He fidgets in his chair.

"I don't justify her cruelty, but too often I see people confined beneath the weight of social expectations. If someone speaks a little louder or reaches a little further to improve one's situation, they're judged. But I care nothing for the social normality. It's why I took you on as an apprentice, to pass on the freedom and power I feel and have embraced. I couldn't allow Eliza or Alfred to take such things away from me or my children. To watch my boys rebel against Alfred—to do what I couldn't do for myself— it showed me what needed to be done concerning Eliza. It's why I did it, Devin. It's why I pulled the trigger. I needed to put an end once and for all to the Culling, no matter what."

His final words make the hairs on the back of my neck prickle. I've always seen Arthur as a gentle man with a kind heart, and now I can add protective to the list.

"You do not need to justify anything to me, sir. I am grateful for my life, though fearful of the unknown, and I will forever be indebted to you. You could have allowed her to kill me, but instead you saved me. I don't think you a villain. I never will." My words resonate within my heart, bringing a strange feeling of fear.

There's a moment of silence before I ask about Alfred. Arthur relaxes, explaining how his brother survived, though remained bedridden for a few days. During the time of his recuperation, Arthur reminded him to never interfere with the business of his family again. After Eliza's funeral, Alfred returned to Hallsent without speaking a word to his brother.

"I'd like to think I've finally earned his respect," Arthur says with a smirk, "but he's outnumbered here, and I'll accept that he's simply admitting defeat."

I ask about the other siblings, and we talk a little more casually. Selene had a few wounds from her fight with Eliza and has recovered to full health. Quintin found Sophia safe and well in the cellar. They didn't stay for the funeral, but returned to the township of Harlic, in the Delova Providence. Arthur paid Quintin his accrued allowance from the previous five years and established a set budget for years to come.

"Quintin and I left on happier terms, though Sophia never spoke a word to anyone. Perhaps Henry was right to question the integrity of a relationship between our kind and a natural born human." He shrugs. "Perhaps Sophia with time will accept Quintin's condition and they still live happily together."

Arthur remains stoic, his eyes still gazing at the floorboards. "Now, when you are recovered from your current situation, I wish for you to tend to Quintin's allowance. What they choose to do with the money is up to them, but you will manage the books of his carpentry business."

"Don't you think such a task would be ideal under your supervision?" I ask.

Arthur shakes his head, folding his arms in his lap. "For now, I think it best for you to learn how one manages one's allowance. I'll be providing a set allowance for you as well, assuming you still wish to *court* my dearest Selene?"

The mention of her quickens my heartbeat. I carefully sit straight. "I do wish court her, with your permission, of course. And though I have no wealth or social station, I will work toward an engagement of marriage, should she still have me for her own."

We look at one another, Arthur's face softening at my humility. "When I became aware of the obvious affections between you two, I expected you to ask for my blessing and permission much sooner." He smiles, chuckling a little to himself. "You have my blessing, Devin. You have my permission to marry Selene after a lengthy courtship, which we will establish once you've fully recovered."

"Thank you, sir."

A knock on the doorframe interrupts our conversation. We look and find Selene standing at the doorway dressed in black from head to toe. I stand as she enters the room and respectfully bow.

"Am I interrupting?" she questions.

"Not at all," I say, catching my breath.

"I should see how Marcus is doing with Diane," Arthur says, smiling. "Do eventually try to rest."

"I will. Thank you, sir."

CHAPTER 30

"You should be lying still beneath the covers," Selene says, pulling away the blanket. Half her hair is pulled up, leaving a few large curls to cascade over her shoulders as she bends to fluff the pillows. Her black satin dress swishes every time she moves.

She waits for me to slip comfortably within the sheets before sitting in the chair her father first occupied. Her dark brown eyes glisten in the sun's light, and though she wears the color of mourning, I'm still enchanted by the sight of her.

"Hattie says you woke in a fright. I wish it was the only unpleasant thing you will have deal with."

I take her hand, kissing the knuckles gently. "As long as I wake from whatever torture awaits me to find you still here in the flesh, I'm willing to endure whatever I must."

Placing a hand upon my forehead, Selene checks for a fever. "I don't believe delirium has set in quite yet. After all you've been through, you still wish to be with me?"

"As long as you wish to have me. Who would I swear my unconditional devotion to when setting out on a new adventure, if not you?"

Our fingers intertwine, and she moves from the chair to sit upon the bed beside me.

Softly she caresses my cheek and says, "I must confess, these past months I've withheld my deepest desires. You've been an open book, entrusting me with things you would never mention to a priest," she says with a smile.

"And I pray you never divulge such things to the local parson. He'd run me out of town if he knew how wild I once was."

We share a chuckle, and she runs her fingers through my fiery red hair. "And should he do so, I will happily join you, for at your side is the only place I wish to be."

She kisses me and stares into my eyes with a tender look. It's a look I've never seen before, one of complete trust and devotion.

"Agreed," I say, glancing at her soft lips.

She makes herself comfortable in my arms, resting her head upon my clothed chest. "I don't think I've ever told you about the thicket across from the yellow poppy fields," she says, tapping her fingertips over my forearm.

She proceeds to describe a well-hidden place where shards of colored glass are hung with twine. Some claim it was where Anna Onway once resided, while others believe a roaming nomad hung the glass in honor of the sunrise. I hold her close as she describes the way the sun hits the glass, creating speckles of colored light, reflecting it on the tree trunks surrounding the mysterious mobile. I'm at ease and filled with peace. Every conversation before had a purpose or some deeper meaning behind it, but now Selene's words lift into the ether, filling my heart with the hope she's finally comfortable enough to be her true self in my presence.

I may not know what lies ahead as for this cursed infection I now have, but I'm not afraid. With the wisdom Arthur possesses and the love from Selene, I trust I'll be all right with whatever challenges come my way. I've survived so far. What could a few more adventures do but encourage me to be a little better, a little braver.

Once Selene finishes her story, I rest my chin upon her soft hair, taking in her scent of lavender and raspberries. "Your father never mentioned what happened to Elara," I say, still feeling a tinge of sadness. "How is she faring with your mother gone?"

Selene shrugs, getting more comfortable in my arms. "As good as she can be. She left a couple days ago. She's headed to the mainland to annul her engagement contract, which she is required to do in person."

I sit up, moving Selene to look at her face. Once again, her words belie a hidden meaning. "You mean she's going to find Keagan. Will she kill him?"

Selene gives me an amused look. "You sound a little frightened. Are you actually worried for the man?"

I hesitate to ask again, in fear of offending Selene, but I must know. "Will she kill him?" I repeat.

My beloved brushes away her hair from off her shoulders. "I don't know, but if he's a threat to the safety of our family, I hope she does. Did he give you any indication of his intentions?"

I don't want to start my life with Selene with secrets, and Keagan is a grown man who understands the consequences of his actions. "He was out of his mind in fear and panic, but he did mention hiring hunters. He's a reasonable man, though. I think with the right incentives, he will protect your secret."

"Our secret," she corrects and waves a dismissive hand. "The family has dealt with hunters before. Living on an island in a small community gives us an advantage of hearing who comes and goes. We'll deal with the threat should it arise."

"Perhaps when she returns, she'll take up again with Harold. I wouldn't mind having my best friend as a brother-by-law." I can't help but think of Harold and the pain he feels not knowing the truth behind Elara's rejection. Besides the obvious curse, Elara is a woman of tradition and societal discipline. I'd like to think, if she manages to return to Anna's Cove, she'll be a changed woman, ready to love as freely as her sister.

"I'm just grateful Elara finally left Addington Manor by her own accord," Selene says. "She never ventures anywhere alone. Perhaps it will be good for her to see the wider world and put Anna's Cove society in its proper perspective."

"One can only hope." I reach out and take hold of one of Selene's curls, twisting it softly around my fingers. "And how are you feeling about how things ended between you and your mother?"

My beloved grows quiet as she thinks to herself. I'm mentally noting what topics to avoid in order to keep her happy, but anger and grief must be expressed, lest they fester.

"She'll always be my mother," Selene says with a tinge of resentment in her tone. "I'm half the woman I am today because of everything she taught me, but unlike Elara, I never shared her ideals on how to act or live my life. I suppose I inherited my father's free spirit and playful heart. But there will always be something to remind me of her, and whether I embrace the memory of her or not is entirely up to me."

She removes my hand from her hair but holds it in both hands. "You should get some rest. I will tend to you as the curse spreads. I wish I could spare you the agony."

"How will I know if it's really you and not some fever dream?"

She smiles and leans closer. Our lips are but a small distance apart. "When the scent of lavender is all you smell, then know your beloved is near, and all is well."

She quotes a passage from a poem written by Theci. The poem speaks of a sailor lost at sea and drifting closer to death. Lavender is the scent of his lover, the last sensation he is aware of before everything goes dark.

Leaning closer, Selene kisses me. I grab her, pulling her

further onto the bed. She squeals and laughs, mischievously snuggling into me under the guise of pushing me away.

"Mr. Foster, if the residents of Anna's Cove were to discover such indecorous actions, everyone would be in a stir," she says, exaggerating her motions and fluttering her eyes.

"You're absolutely right, Miss Selene, but I say let them talk." I tease, mimicking her mannerisms.

I'm overcome with a thought as I'm lost in the deep pools of her eyes. "Do you believe the residents of Anna's Cove can handle an impoverished apprentice courting an Addington daughter?"

Kissing me once again, she wraps her arms around my neck and holds me tightly.

"I'd think it romantic and rather exciting. Let the old fools whisper and the silly hens cluck. Everything will be just fine between the two of us."

Again, she rests at my side, settling in so completely I'm not even sure she intends to leave once I've fallen asleep.

As I rest with my beloved in my arms, I slowly lower my eyelids, unsure of what will become of me. The secrets I will hold. The things I will never tell. Poor Harold, if only he could know what his encouragement has led me to. If only Ms. Taylor could know how I have now become part of her narrative. I have become part of the whispers of Addington Manor.

THE END

ACKNOWLEDGMENTS

I want to begin this with a much needed thanks to my amazing husband and best friend. Thank you for your endless support and pep talks whenever I was overwhelmed with self-doubt or met with unfamiliar challenges. Your analytical eye and ability to see hidden potential is astounding. I couldn't have finished this book without your encouragement and tough love.

I want to thank my sweet children. You have a way of inspiring me and remind me how I'm not alone in this journey. Thanks for your patience whenever I needed to finalize revisions. Thanks for the many hugs and late-night chats; you're all awesome and I hope you keep developing what you're most passionate about in life.

Of course, I must thank my wonderful family. From a young age you were always giving me time to develop my strange little hobby into the dream I am now living. Now as an adult, I'm grateful for the moments of sharing my dreams of writing and still being met with the sincerest support. Thanks for your interest in what matters most to me.

And lastly, I wanted to thank everyone who took the time to join me on this wonderful adventure. Whether you were listening to my ramblings of plot development, world building, character insights or momentary bragging about my hopes and aspirations—thank you for your patience and listening ear. I want to give a shoutout to my awesome beta readers: Cristina, Ashley, Mallorie, Kaylee, Amy, and all the others who wish to remain anonymous. All of you have sincerely touched my life in a way you will never comprehend. Your amazing feedback, cute comments, editorial insights, and compliments have buoyed me through the rough waters of revisions and personal vulnerability. Thank you now and forever for taking time to read my words.

ABOUT THE AUTHOR

Living within the western shadow of the Rocky Mountains, M. E. Hansen is a cross genre author and lover of all things supernatural, fantastical and romantic. When she's not getting excited about the next plot twist in her latest book, she's running a house full of monkeys, taming a vicious Norwegian Forest cat, and falling endlessly in love with her ingenious do-gooder of a husband.